I AM
SIN

I AM SIN

HELEN HARDT

WATERHOUSE PRESS

This book is an original publication of Waterhouse Press.

This is a work of fiction. Names, characters, places, and incidents either are the product of the author's imagination or are used fictitiously, and any resemblance to actual persons, living or dead, business establishments, events, or locales is entirely coincidental. The publisher does not assume any responsibility for third-party websites or their content.

Copyright © 2024 Waterhouse Press, LLC
Cover Design by Waterhouse Press, LLC
Cover Images: Shutterstock

All Rights Reserved.
No part of this book may be reproduced, scanned, or distributed in any printed or electronic format without permission. Please do not participate in or encourage piracy of copyrighted materials in violation of the author's rights. Purchase only authorized editions.

ISBN: 978-1-64263-408-2

To all my fans—
thank you so much for your friendship and support!

PROLOGUE

DRAGON

For the first nine years of my life, there was light. There was love. There was kindness.

And then, in the course of one evening, that light was eclipsed forever.

Since then, I've lived in a chasm of darkness.

It hasn't been all bad. Over the years, I've been able to escape some of the obscurity. I've learned to live my life in the dusk. I found my way to Jesse Pike, a man who not only saw the darkness in me but embraced it. He needed a drummer. I was a drummer. His band had no name. He liked my name, so he used it for the band.

But of course, I went and fucked that up.

Because of the darkness. The black cloud that follows me everywhere I go, perpetually wrapping me in a fog of rain and hail.

That night, the shadows overtook me. I chose to combat it with more darkness. A quick hit of black tar. I threw years of sobriety down the toilet, all because I couldn't control the dark Dragon within me.

Because I am sin. I am the purest entity of evil. I must be.

Why else would my parents—?

No. I can't think about that. Thinking like that is what

caused my relapse.

But it's true.

The Dragon was not born into it, but he will live his life in his own black smoke.

And that's where he'll die, too.

CHAPTER ONE

DIANA

I let out an exasperated sigh. "I just don't think it's a good idea, Brianna."

"I wouldn't ask you if it weren't so important to Jesse and me," my younger sister, newly married to the man of her dreams—a rising rock star, no less—pleads. "He wants to be close to his rehab place in case he relapses."

I bite my lip. "He was fine at your wedding. I didn't see him take a drink at all, and he stood there solidly as Jesse's best man."

"Yes, exactly. He wants to *stay* fine." Brianna sighs. "There won't be any band business for the next several months, and he wants to be in Denver, close to his therapist and to the facility."

I put the phone on speaker and set it on the counter. I rub both sides of my forehead, trying to think this through. I'm not one to turn down a person in need, but this is a lot to ask of anyone. House a recovering addict? A guy I hardly know? Sure, he's the drummer for my brother-in-law's band, but he and I have barely said ten words to each other.

Plus, I just moved into my plush penthouse here in downtown Denver. I'm about to begin the job of my dreams. Call me selfish, but I kind of want to focus on me at the moment.

"I'll think about it. That's all I'll say."

"Think fast, will you? He's arriving in Denver tomorrow."

I let out a huff as I say goodbye to my sister and end the call.

Today is Friday, and I begin as an associate architect with Lund & Lopez here in Denver on Monday. I completed an internship at a different firm, and they made me an offer, but the two Ls came in a little bit higher.

But that's not the reason I went with L & L. I don't need the money. I have a sizable trust fund from my rich family. I went with L & L because they just got a huge contract to build a new eco-resort on top of one of the highest peaks in the Rockies. It's a project like no other, and I'm hoping I'll get to be involved.

To win a spot on that team, I'll have to show the higher-ups in the firm that I'm someone serious about my architecture career who's ready to put in the time on this amazing project. That I'm not just some heiress trying to prove a point.

I need to be focused.

Letting a recovering addict live in my penthouse isn't a good way to stay focused.

I look around. Do I even have the room?

Of course I do. I have three bedrooms, all with en suite bathrooms.

But I only have one kitchen, one common area. One balcony with a view of the Rocky Mountains to the west.

I've lived alone since I was twenty-one. I'm nearly twenty-six now, and the thought of taking a roommate—especially one with so much baggage—kind of makes me want to hurl.

Brianna and Jesse offered to pay rent for him. I don't need the extra income, of course, so I said no. He can pay his own damned rent.

His name is Dragon.

Yes, that's really his name. Dragon Locke. He's the drummer for Jesse's rock band, Dragonlock. They liked his name so much they named the band after him.

I've spoken to him a few times at gatherings back home at my family's ranch on the western slope of Colorado. Usually just small talk. The weather, the wedding decor, what the band's working on.

He's rock-star gorgeous, complete with the long hair and stubble and dark sexiness.

But when I say dark, I don't just mean his hair.

Dragon has a darkness that exudes from his pores, as if there's something inside him that I don't fully trust.

Brianna and Jesse would never put me in harm's way. I trust my sister, and she and Jesse know Dragon better than I ever could, but he's always seemed a little bit dangerous to me.

And I *don't* want him living in my home.

I'm going to have to call Brianna back and tell her I've made a decision. That I'm sorry, but he'll have to stay somewhere else. If they're willing to pay for his rent, they can easily find another place in Denver. Maybe even one closer to his rehab center. No reason why I need to be involved at all. Why my life needs to be disrupted as I'm starting a new career. Why I even have to be thinking about this.

I pick up my phone to call my sister when a knock on the door startles me. Probably just maintenance or something. Anyone else would have buzzed up.

I walk to the door and look through my peephole.

You've got to be kidding me.

It's him.

Dragon Locke.

His gorgeous hair falls in waves around his broad shoulders, and his long-lashed hazel eyes stare straight at me.

It should be a sin for someone to be so good-looking. I grew up with a rash of handsome brothers and cousins, so I'm no stranger to gorgeous men.

Dragon Locke—even with the darkness that seems to enshroud him—makes them all look like hamburger meat.

How the hell did he even get in here?

"Who is it?" I ask, even though I know very well who it is.

"Dragon. Dragon Locke."

The rich timbre of his voice makes me shiver. "How did you get in here?"

"I followed an Uber Eats guy in."

I roll my eyes. Great. That's the problem with buzzing up. In this day and age of app deliveries, anyone can just waltz right in.

"What do you want?"

"Just to talk, Diana."

I swallow. "Bree said you weren't coming into town until tomorrow."

"Change of plans."

He's a man of few words, but I already knew that.

No one really knows much about Dragon. He's a recovering addict, and he had a relapse about nine months ago when the band was in Europe opening for Emerald Phoenix. He wasn't able to complete the tour. He returned to Denver, got into a concentrated rehab program, and was well enough to stand up as Jesse's best man for the wedding a week ago.

That's all I know—other than the fact that his stare through my thick wooden door has me quivering—and not in a frightened way.

Another thing I don't need.

"Fine. Come on in." I open the door.

CHAPTER TWO

DRAGON

To say Diana Steel is beautiful is like saying the Rocky Mountains are beautiful.

They are, no doubt, but they're also so much more.

The Rockies are majestic and awe-inspiring. It's hard to put into words just how breathtaking they are to someone who hasn't seen them in person. Towering peaks, rugged cliffs, and a sea of evergreen trees as far as the eye can see. Blue and purple from a distance, but green and lush as you get nearer. Reddish rocks that hide faces and other images in their depths. Snow-capped peaks where sunlight sparkles.

Diana Steel is a different kind of wonder. Her dark hair cascades in silken waves—a deep hue that gleams like polished mahogany. It frames her face with an air of mystery, casting shadows and highlights that dance with each graceful movement.

But her hair pales in comparison to her dark eyes. They're like deep, endless lakes—windows into her soul. They're magnetic, and they draw me in. They lock onto mine, and I don't ever want to look away.

"Are you going to stand there staring, or are you going to tell me what you want?"

Her voice jolts me back to reality.

All the Steel women are beautiful, but Diana has a gentleness about her that some of the others don't. She's the opposite of her sister, Brianna, who's a spitfire of a cowgirl. Even at her wedding to my best friend, Jesse Pike, her personality shone through her traditional western dress.

"Thanks for letting me in."

She scratches her arm. "Bree told me you weren't coming until tomorrow."

Did she forget she already said that through the door? "I hadn't planned to," I say, "but it was a gorgeous day for a drive. The aspens have turned, and I don't know... I just felt like coming."

She furrows her brow. "And I suppose you need a place to stay."

I shake my head. "That's actually what I stopped by to talk to you about. This whole thing wasn't my idea, Diana. I hope you know that."

"All I know is that Brianna says it's important that you stay here."

"I've got a hotel booked for tonight, and I've got enough in savings to stay there for the next couple of weeks if I have to." I frown. "That should be plenty of time to find another... situation."

She blinks, her face stiff. "All right."

"I don't know if you're even considering their request," I say, "but if you are, I wanted to stop by and tell you it's not necessary."

"Okay, Dragon." She sighs. "It's not that I don't want to help you. It's just that—"

I walk toward her and quiet her by holding up a hand. "You don't have to give me any reasons or excuses or anything." I look down, kicking at the marble-tiled floor. "I know someone like you doesn't want to have someone like me encroaching on her space."

She narrows her eyes at me. "Now you wait just a minute. I never said anything about who you are or anything like that."

I can't help a scoff. "Give me a break, Diana. You're a member of the Steel family. You're about as high class as they get. And I'm..."

She whips her hands to her hips. "You're what, exactly?"

I don't reply. I don't talk about myself. Not the present, and especially not the past. Not to anyone. Jesse is the only one—other than my therapist—I've trusted with it, and even he doesn't know everything. But he's kept my confidence. Even when I betrayed him big time and fell off the wagon during the band's big break, he forgave me.

"Are you going to answer me?" Diana insists.

"No," I say flatly.

"I hate it when people do this." She balls her hands into fists, her cheeks and neck turning red. "People assume just because I was born into privilege that I don't understand anybody else. That I think people are beneath me. I'm not like that, Dragon. None of my family is. You should know that by now."

Her beauty has turned fiery. Maybe I misjudged her. Maybe she's as much of a spitfire as her sister, and damn...

This woman is so out of my league. God knows I'm still too fucked up for any kind of relationship, but everything in me wants me to grab her, kiss her, throw her over my shoulder, take her into her bedroom, and fuck the living daylights out of her.

Hard, fast, and not gentle.

Because *I'm* not gentle.
But Diana Steel is not for me.
She's beauty and light personified, and I...
I ruin everything I touch.

CHAPTER THREE

DIANA

"Get out, then," I say, "if you're not going to answer me. You've told me why you're here. For some reason, you felt the need to tell me none of this was your idea."

"It wasn't," he says.

"And clearly you think I'm some kind of stuck-up snob who wouldn't want the likes of you staying with me anyway."

He shrugs. "You haven't told me I'm wrong."

"Oh!" I turn around, pace a few steps away from the door, and then turn back. "This kind of stuff drives me insane. Do you think I'm here in Denver for my health? I'm here because I want a career in architecture. I'm not working for the family business. I want my own damned life."

"Did I say you didn't?"

"No. You simply insinuated that I wouldn't want you staying with me because I'm some little rich girl who doesn't want to be bothered with the dregs of society."

He chuckles then, which is odd, because I'm not sure I've ever seen Dragon Locke laugh.

"What the hell is so funny?" I demand.

"You're contradicting your own point," he says. "I never said I was the dregs of society. Those words came out of your mouth."

"You specifically said *'someone like me.'*"

He exhales sharply through his nose. "Pretty vague on my part. You filled in the blanks."

I open my mouth to offer a retort, but he lifts a hand to quiet me.

"And frankly, I don't have a problem with that." He looks around the apartment. "I don't have a problem with any of this. Like I said, none of it was my idea. I'm here, I have a hotel room for the night, and I won't be bothering you anymore. Forget that Jesse and Brianna even asked you to do this favor. It's not necessary. It was never necessary."

He turns, but I grab his arm, forcing him to face me. "It really doesn't matter what you think of me."

"I couldn't agree more, Diana." Then he leaves, closing the door behind him.

Good. Good riddance.

I need to make myself some dinner anyway. I had an early lunch, and my stomach was growling before Dragon showed up.

Funny. I'm not that hungry now.

Still, I traipse into my kitchen—my huge gourmet kitchen.

It's twice the size of the kitchen I shared with my roommates when I was in college. Ample counter space—granite, of course. Rich cabinets of dark wood, half of which are empty or holding a few dishes at most. A mammoth island in the middle that's big enough to house a five-burner gas range, a second sink—yes, I have two—and a small wine fridge. Top-of-the-line appliances, the crown jewel of which is my professional-grade refrigerator.

I could easily handle two people using this kitchen. Maybe I *am* the selfish bitch that I accused Dragon of calling me. I sigh and open my refrigerator.

I grab the pound of ground beef that I took out to defrost yesterday. My family is in the beef business, so I eat a lot of beef. I'll fry myself a burger, and I'll have leftovers for tomorrow.

And for some reason, without thinking—

I head back to the door, open it, and dart my gaze down the hallway.

Dragon stands, waiting for the elevator.

"Dragon?"

He turns and raises his dark eyebrows.

"I'm making myself a burger. There's too much for just me. Do you want one?"

He cocks his head.

Doesn't say anything.

"Do you think that's a trick question?" I ask.

He walks toward me. When he gets to the door, he simply says, "Sure."

For a second, I think he's replying to my trick question comment, but he's actually accepting my dinner invitation.

I can't house him, but I can at least feed him. Maybe it will show him that I'm not some horrible heiress who can't bother herself to help someone in need.

Because frankly, Dragon is not in *need*. He's a member of Dragonlock, an up-and-coming rock band that I know is going to make it big. And he has access to Jesse's wallet, so he doesn't need to stay here. He can easily find another place.

I mean seriously. Why did it have to be *here*? With me?

None of that makes any sense at all.

"What do you like on your burger?" I ask as I head back into the kitchen.

"Everything," he says.

I purse my lips. "Okay, that doesn't tell me shit. I've got lettuce, tomato, onion, avocado, ketchup, mustard, mayo. Cheddar cheese, smoked Gouda, pepper jack."

He nods. "Sounds great."

I raise an eyebrow. "You're not telling me you want all of that on your burger."

"That's what I'm saying."

"Three different kinds of cheese?"

He shrugs. "Uh...yeah. I'm pretty sure you understand English."

I roll my eyes and turn back toward the kitchen. "Fine."

I take the ground beef and form it into four quarter-pound burgers. "You want a double?"

"Yeah, sounds great."

I fry three of the burgers, saving the fourth for my lunch tomorrow, on a cast-iron grill pan while I slice some tomato, onion, and avocado.

I pull two of my cousin Ava's—she's a gourmet baker in our small hometown of Snow Creek, Colorado—brioche buns out of the freezer and put them in the toaster.

The savory scent of beef fills my penthouse. It's a comforting scent, a familiar scent. Reminds me of being at home when I was a kid, hanging with Brianna and our two older brothers, Dale and Donny.

Dragon is still standing in the foyer.

"You can sit down," I tell him.

He nods and walks toward my small kitchen table. He lifts his eyebrows.

"Anywhere is fine," I say.

He nods again and takes a seat—right in the chair I usually use, but whatever.

The buns pop out of the toaster, and I set each of them on a plate, dousing them with ketchup, mustard, and mayo, though I skip the mayo on my own. Once the burgers are done, I lay a slice of cheese on Dragon's bun, place a burger on top of it, and then top the second patty with the remaining two slices of cheese. I swear to God, my stomach gurgles as I do it. That's way more cheese than I can eat at one time. I'd be spending the evening in the bathroom. I finish with lettuce, tomato, onion, and avocado, place a handful of potato chips on the side, and take the plate over to him.

"What would you like to drink?"

"Water's fine."

"You sure? I have diet soft drinks and iced tea."

"Water," he repeats.

Okay, then.

I grab a glass out of my cupboard, fill it with ice and water from the door of my refrigerator, and take it to Dragon along with a napkin.

When he doesn't eat, I say, "Go ahead. I'll be here in a minute."

I assemble my own burger with only one slice of cheese— the Gouda—and sit down opposite Dragon at my small table.

He takes a bite, chews, swallows, and then wipes his chin with his napkin. "Good," he says.

"Glad you like it." I take a bite of my own burger.

It's good. Delicious, actually. My family raises the best beef in the nation. Even our ground beef, which is made from the less-expensive cuts, is tastier than most non-Steel filet mignon. It's all grass-fed, which gives it a richer flavor.

Dragon doesn't talk as he eats, and I start to feel a little awkward.

Okay. A lot awkward.

Why did I invite him in here for dinner again? Just to prove some stupid point about me not being a big snob?

I like to savor my food. I don't like to eat too quickly. Everyone in my family was raised to appreciate food—the fact that it's art as well as sustenance. Each flavor and texture is something to be discovered and enjoyed. Even something as simple as a burger.

But tonight? I snarf down the burger as if I haven't eaten in weeks. The sooner we're both done, the sooner I can escort Dragon back to the door and end this unease.

Once I'm finished, I pick up my plate and take it over to the kitchen.

Dragon still has a few chips on his plate, but he makes no move to eat them. I return to the table and gesture to his plate. "Done?"

"Not quite."

Crap.

"Okay. You want anything else? More chips?" I glance at his empty glass. "More water?"

He shakes his head slowly. "I'm good."

God, what is *with* this guy? Every other man I know can eat an entire bag of potato chips in one sitting. Growing up with two brothers, I was lucky if I ever even got a chip on the rare occasions my mother brought any into the house. And they weren't awkwardly invading someone's personal space when they were doing so. But Dragon seems to have no qualms about how odd I find his presence. He makes no move to eat the last few chips.

There's only one thing I can think of to fill the silence.

"Dessert, then? I have some ice cream in the freezer."

Damn it, why did I just say that? He'll probably take an hour to get through a bowl of ice cream.

"Not much of a sweet tooth," he says.

I blink, slightly grateful for his rejection. "All right." I walk back to the kitchen. "I'll just clean up a little, then."

"Yeah. Whatever." He stares at his plate. "Pretend I'm not here."

I wrinkle my brow. Seriously? He just said that?

I grab a scouring pad for the cast iron and get to work. With the water still running, I rinse the plates and load them in the dishwasher. When I turn off the faucet, a faint humming drifts toward me.

Interesting tune. Kind of sad, and not one I've heard before.

"What's that?" I ask.

Dragon turns toward me. "What?"

"You're humming."

He lifts his eyebrows. "I was?"

"Yeah. Is this a new song the band is working on?"

"No."

"It's really beautiful. Sounds kind of...sad."

"I'm afraid I don't really know what you're talking about."

"You were definitely humming, Dragon."

He frowns. "Yeah, I probably was. I fiddle around with tunes in my head, but none of them are good enough for the band."

I take a few steps toward him. "Why would you say that?"

"Because Jesse and Cage are both musical geniuses. They write most of the music and lyrics. They've never asked for my input."

"Have you *offered* your input?"

He shakes his head quickly. "Why would I? They both have degrees in music. I don't even have—" He stops abruptly.

"You don't even have what?"

"Nothing." He rises. "The burger was great. What do I owe you?"

I drop my jaw. "You really didn't just ask me that question."

"Relax. I'm kidding. I appreciate the meal."

For the love of God, what was I thinking, inviting him to eat with me? And what am I thinking now? This is all on me. I invited him for dinner. He simply came by to tell me I didn't need to let him stay with me.

So why do I feel this strange obligation?

"Fine," I say.

He stares ahead. "Fine what?"

I wave my hands. "You can stay here, okay? There's plenty of room, and I'll be at the office most of my waking hours anyway. So why not?"

He wrinkles his forehead. "Where is all this coming from?"

"You obviously think I'm some kind of stuck-up person who has a huge penthouse but doesn't want to share."

He furrows his brow. "You've got me all wrong, Diana."

He's right. I'm reading all kinds of things into this. I've just always hated it when people make assumptions about me based on my family's wealth.

"I honestly just came by to let you know I'm in town," he continues, "and to tell you that I have no intention of asking for—"

"Just stop it. I said you can stay."

"I've already checked into my hotel. My stuff is all there."

"Then come back tomorrow. You can move in then."

"Diana—"

"Look. This will make my sister happy. It will make her new husband happy."

"But it's not going to make you happy."

I blink for a few seconds before responding. "I'll deal. Like I said, I'm starting my first real job as an architect on Monday. I need to make a good impression, which means I need to put in a lot of hours at the office. I'll hardly be here."

He shrugs. "All right."

Seriously? He's not even going to offer me a thank-you?

He walks to the door and then turns once again, meeting my gaze.

His eyes are beautiful—a gorgeous gold and green with long black lashes—but I've never seen them look happy.

And he should be happy now.

He's sober, and his band is doing great things. They opened for Emerald Phoenix during the recent European tour, and even though Dragon was only present for one performance, he's still a member of the band, and he'll join them on future ventures. The tour was a smash, and Dragonlock is on their way.

I wait for Dragon to speak, but he doesn't. He simply looks at me for a few seconds, nods, and then walks out the door.

CHAPTER FOUR

DRAGON

I asked my parents once, after I started kindergarten, why they had named me Dragon. Some of the kids in the class made fun of my name—said it wasn't a real name.

"The same reason we named your sister Griffin," my mother told me. "I've always loved mythological creatures."

I'm not sure how the conversation went after that. No doubt I asked her about mythological creatures and what they were. But I don't remember anything past that.

Because I don't let myself think about Griffin.

I was four years old when Griffin was born, and she was blond and beautiful like my mother. I favored my father, with dark hair, but instead of his brown eyes, mine were what my mother called hazel. She said they were beautiful, and that I was her golden Dragon.

I was so happy to be loved by two doting parents. Parents who cherished me for everything I was.

Until, of course, they turned their backs on me.

When I was nine years old, I became a ward of the state and went to live in a group home.

And Griffin?

She vanished a couple of months later. I don't know how or why, and I didn't know about it when it happened. I was in the group home, and I wasn't informed of her disappearance until years after the fact.

The only person I've trusted with some of my backstory is Jesse Pike, Diana's brother-in-law.

And even he doesn't know the worst of it.

But I have to admit, when he and Brianna came to me with the notion of my staying with Diana, I didn't hate the idea.

Diana Steel is the embodiment of everything good in the world. She's beautiful and intelligent, with a softness that is my complete opposite.

Being in her presence is like being surrounded by a halo of goodness. An inner light that could never allow itself to be enveloped by the shadows of my past. I certainly never expected her to go along with it, and I wanted her to know that there were no hard feelings. That's why I stopped by her place tonight—to tell her that I had no intention of living with her, that I would be fine on my own.

I'm not sure what made her change her mind.

She seemed to think I was insinuating that she wasn't a generous soul, that she didn't want to help someone like me. That's not what I thought at all. It's not what *I think*.

I won't lie, though. I'm glad she changed her mind. Not because her penthouse is more luxurious than any hotel room I can afford, but because being near her goodness...

I don't know.

Maybe some of it will rub off on me.

Not that I'm a bad person.

Despite what my parents thought—and probably still think—of me.

I did not do what they accused me of.

I would never have harmed Griffin.

I loved her. I'm not sure I've ever loved anyone the way I loved my little sister. She was a blond-haired, blue-eyed angel, and I adored her.

I stop my thoughts abruptly.

I'm sober. And when I think of Griffin, I want to drink. I want to shoot up. I want to do everything I can to escape reality.

Because my reality is one without Griffin.

Someone hurt her all those years ago.

And I was blamed for it.

I wake the next day in my hotel room. I can't say that I'm happy—I'm never happy—but I'm content knowing that I'll be staying with Diana Steel. Funny thing is I don't even have her number. I could easily get it from Jesse and Brianna, but I don't.

Part of me wants to just show up. If I call her, that will give her a chance to change her mind.

Seriously, why would she want me staying with her? I don't think she does. She's just doing this out of the goodness of her heart. And to prove that she's not a heartless bitch, I suppose.

I pack up my few belongings, and then I head downstairs to the dining room where I grab a plate of the free breakfast—a croissant, a couple of sausage links, and a portion of scrambled eggs.

Once I take a seat, I look at the croissant. It's crescent-shaped, my favorite phase of the moon. I could've eaten my fill of croissants during the band's stay in Paris, but instead, I chose the easy way out.

Drugs.

I took two groupies to my hotel room, and they offered me heroin. I said no.

They sucked my dick.

And one of them...

One of them had a tattoo of a griffin on her backside.

I thought I could handle it.

Turns out I couldn't.

So I shot up. Got high. Rode the fucking dragon. My tox report showed fentanyl and Rohypnol, so God only knows what else I put into my veins that night.

I fucked up years of sobriety in the middle of the band's big break.

I wasn't sure Jesse would ever forgive me, but he did. He even forgave me enough to let me be his best man when he married Brianna.

I didn't deserve his forgiveness, and I certainly don't deserve to be staying at Diana's house.

But my therapist always says not to feel guilty when someone offers me something. That I'm worthy. That I deserve it.

I still don't believe him, but I am taking it. I'm taking it for selfish reasons.

Because I want to be near Diana Steel.

She's beautiful, of course, and I won't deny my extreme attraction to her, but that's not what this is about.

This is about me surrounding myself with good. It's about me having a place to stay so maybe I won't be tempted to go to a bar...or worse.

I finish my breakfast, grab my duffel, and head to Diana's.

CHAPTER FIVE

DIANA

I have two spare bedrooms in my penthouse. One is a little bit larger, so I like to save it for when family members come to visit.

The other is smaller, but it still has an en suite bathroom and a queen-size bed. The problem is the bedspread is pink, and Dragon Locke is decidedly not a pink kind of person.

I feel like I should redecorate it in black and concrete. Something that matches the color of Dragon's aura, as my cousin Ava would say.

Luckily, the bedspread is the only pink thing in the room. The rest of the items are pretty neutral—light oak furnishings, including the headboard, and two off-white armchairs upholstered in velvet. This is also the room where I display my eclectic collection of art that I've collected during my travels.

There's a beautiful painting of a carousel coming to life that I bought in Saint Louis, a bold print of a turquoise octopus I purchased in Virginia Beach, and an exquisite photograph taken over beach umbrellas in multiple colors that I got when I was visiting Sarasota, Florida. I doubt that Dragon has much of an eye for art, but—

I stop myself. He's literally in a band. I caught him humming a tune of his own composition when he was having dinner here last night. If any man I've met would have an eye for art, it might just be Dragon Locke.

Not that Dragon is a man that I would...

I shake the thoughts out of my head. I remove the pink bedspread, fold it up, and store it in the linen closet. I'll order a new comforter in some neutral color, but for now, I take a brown fleece blanket out of the closet and put it over the bed. I wish I had something black, but brown will have to do for now.

Everything else is in order. I even have shampoo, conditioner, and toothpaste in the bathroom for guests.

Now I just have to wait until he gets here. I don't have his number, so I can't call him. I don't want to call him anyway.

He's so difficult to talk to.

I stand in the doorway and take a look around the room. At the oak nightstand, the driftwood lamp, the tall dresser, the walk-in closet.

It's not perfect, but it will do.

Especially considering that Dragon is staying here for free. If he were staying with any other friend, he'd have a couch to sleep on at best.

Then I glance at the door.

It only has an indoor lock, which I think is fine for him.

But I'll have a key lock on my own door by the end of the day. Anyone can open an indoor lock with one of those little tools, and it's not that I don't trust Dragon. I don't think he's a rapist or a murderer. I wouldn't allow him to stay here if I did.

But the fact is that I don't know him, so I'll be cautious.

I head back to the kitchen and grab my phone from the counter to call maintenance for my building.

"Maintenance," a voice says.

"Hi, this is Diana Steel in the penthouse. I'd like someone

to come up today and install a key lock—no, make that a digital lock—on my bedroom door."

"Of course, Ms. Steel. I can have someone there by two p.m."

"Perfect. Thank you."

I end the call and—

My intercom buzzes.

Can't be Dragon already. It's barely past nine a.m.

"Yes?" I say into the intercom.

"Morning, Diana. It's me."

His husky, low voice sends a shiver through me. I steady myself and lean into the intercom. "You're early."

"I can come back later if you want."

"No, it's okay." I clear my throat. "Come on up." I push the button to open the door.

Good thing I was up early and got his room ready.

I suppose the next thing is to call security and let them know I'll have someone else living here. He'll need a key that will work for my place and the front entrance.

I sigh.

I hope this isn't a big mistake.

The only reason I offered him my apartment in the first place was because he insinuated that I wouldn't want to be associating with the likes of him. Because I've been constantly scrutinized because of the privilege I was born into, I immediately went on the defensive and assumed he was calling me an uppity bitch. So, to prove that I wasn't, I did the "logical" thing and opened my home up to a complete stranger.

Well, *almost* complete stranger.

I take a seat on my couch and enjoy my final moments of total privacy.

A few moments later, he knocks on the door.

I open it. His long dark hair is pulled back into a low ponytail this morning. I force back a chuckle. Rock stars and their long hair. I don't get long hair on men. My brother Dale wears his hair long, and his wife loves it. Most women do. But long hair on a man has never been my thing.

Except on Dragon. I have the strange urge to pull the band out of his hair and watch it flow over his broad shoulders.

And damn...he has *broad* shoulders.

He's only about six feet tall, which is short to me since my father and brothers are all over six two, but his mere presence makes him seem bigger.

I open the door and gesture for him to come in.

He carries a medium-sized duffel bag—camouflage print—and a backpack. That's it.

Imagine having everything you own in only two bags.

"I'll show you to your room," I say.

He nods and follows me.

I open the door. "It locks from the inside so you can have some privacy while you're in here. You've got a queen-size bed, and here's your en suite bathroom with a tub and shower. There's some shampoo and toothpaste in here, but you'll need to get the rest of the stuff yourself."

He nods again.

I swallow, cross the room, and open the door to the closet. "And here's your closet."

He drops his jaw. "A walk-in closet?"

"Yeah."

"Fuck," he says. "I've never had one."

"Well, you do now." Though I doubt he has enough clothes in those two bags to fill it.

His eyes are wide, but his face remains motionless. "This is great."

"Glad you like it." I inch toward the hallway. "Go ahead and get settled in. I assume you'll get your own groceries and make your own meals. I've cleared off a shelf in the pantry, and I'll do one in the fridge for you."

"I appreciate it."

"Not a problem." I turn and start to leave.

He clears his throat. "So about compensation."

My heart flutters. Why is every conversation with this man so unsettling?

I turn around and paste a smile on my face. "Don't worry about that. You just concentrate on staying sober, and you'll of course be responsible for your own meals and toiletries."

He frowns. "I've got to pay something, Diana."

I blink. "What can you afford?"

He takes a deep breath and fixes his eyes on the floor. "Well, not much at the moment. But I plan to start taking private students for drumming. And then of course, once Jesse and Rory are both back from their honeymoons, the band will start performing again."

"Then let's just leave it for now." I turn again, but I stop. I crane my neck back into the room. "By the way... Where exactly are you planning to take students?"

"Not here. Don't worry."

I look around. "Where are your drums?"

He takes another deep breath and looks out the window toward the mountains. "They're still at the Pike place, in the garage. If I get any students, I'll rent a studio and drums here in the city."

I nod. "Good enough."

"That's what I've been doing anyway. You know, to practice."

"Good."

That means he has enough money to at least do that. Brianna told me that all the band members got a signing bonus of ten thousand dollars when they agreed to open for Emerald Phoenix in the UK and Europe, but I doubt Dragon was compensated much after that since he only performed once. They had to bring in a substitute drummer.

"Okay, then." I place my hand on the doorknob. "Go ahead and get settled. I'm going to go down and talk to security about getting some keys for you. We use key cards here. You'll have one for the main building so you don't have to use the intercom every time you want to come up, and it will also get you into this penthouse."

"One key for both?"

I clear my throat. "Yeah. We're on the cutting edge of technology here." I regret the words as soon as I speak them. They sounded pretty condescending.

But he doesn't seem to take offense.

"I appreciate it," he says again.

"You're welcome," I say with a little bite in my voice.

His eyebrow twitches, but he doesn't say anything. He just leans down and opens one of his duffels.

I shake my head and leave the room.

CHAPTER SIX

DRAGON

I walk back toward the large window. I have an amazing view—much better than my room at the hotel.

There's a TV and a remote. A small desk set up for a computer. I don't have a computer, but I do have a phone. It's my computer for now. I noticed there was a computer in the living area off to the side—a little alcove Diana probably uses as a home office.

Maybe Diana will let me use her computer.

I don't know, though, and I wouldn't ask her anyway.

This is all so strange.

I look around the room. Diana has some interesting art on the wall. I'm drawn to a print of a greenish-blue octopus, its tentacles waving in opposite directions. I empathize with the creature. I too feel pulled in multiple directions at once.

Maybe I should have just gone back home to the western slope. But my therapist was right. Being close to him as well as the rehab facility gives me a safety net if things go wrong.

But should I *really* be staying with Diana? My best friend's sister-in-law?

If we had grown up together, were as close as Jesse and I are, then I'd have no problem crashing at her place for a few weeks or even longer if I were paying rent or buying groceries.

I'm not even doing that. She doesn't need the money, of course. The Steels are loaded, and she apparently has this great job lined up.

Still, something just doesn't feel right about this.

I could be happy here. I *want* to be happy here.

I can't dwell on that right now. First thing I need to do is get some groceries. I take a few minutes to unpack—that's all it takes because I have so few belongings—and then I walk out. Diana's in the kitchen putting away groceries.

"Do you want some help?"

"No, that's not necessary. I'm just clearing off a shelf for you in the refrigerator. You won't need more than one shelf, will you?"

I shrug. "I'll make do. I figured I'd go out and get some groceries. Where do you normally shop?"

"I don't have time to shop," she says. "I have all my groceries delivered. I can give you the info if you'd like."

I can barely afford the groceries the way my finances are right now, let alone the delivery fees and a courier tip.

"No, I feel like getting out."

"Good enough. I'll have to buzz you up, though. At least until I can get down to security and get your key."

"That's fine." I leave the penthouse and walk to the elevator.

There's a grocery store near my rehab center. That's where I'm used to doing my shopping. I really only asked Diana where she shopped to make conversation. I'm not one to worry about conversation in general, but for some reason, I want to talk to her. Even about something as mundane as her favorite grocery store.

I arrive at the market, walk in, and grab a basket. No cart

since I'll have to walk back. I grab a couple loaves of bread, cold cuts for sandwiches, a few condiments, and some eggs and bacon. Last is produce. Apples and pears and some celery and carrot sticks. One bag of potato chips and that should do me for the week. I pay with cash, leaving me with about two hundred dollars.

In my bank account, I have about two grand left from my bonus. That's it. I don't know why I was thinking I could pay Diana rent. As the words left my mouth, I knew I'd be royally screwed if she actually took me up on the offer. Renting a room in her high-class penthouse would be at least two grand a month, which would wipe me out.

If I can't find any percussion students, I'll have to get a job until the band is back in business, and that's at least two months away because Jesse and Rory are both taking long-ass honeymoons.

Not that I begrudge them that. They've earned it. Their amazing dual-lead vocals are why the band did so well in Europe. It certainly wasn't because of me. I wasn't there.

I fucked up and had to go to rehab.

Frankly, I'm lucky they're all still speaking to me.

I load my groceries into two reusable bags and walk back to Diana's building. Once I make it to the entrance, I press the intercom for her penthouse.

"Yes?" Her voice comes through loud and clear.

"It's me, Dragon. I got my groceries."

"Great." The door clicks open.

I walk in through the lobby and to the elevators. I'll look around later today once I get a key. To the right is what looks like an amazing fitness center. I should probably make use of it if I can.

I wait for the elevator along with an elderly couple who look me up and down.

I'm sure they're taking in my black army boots, camouflage coat, and faded blue jeans. And of course my long hair.

Probably not the kind of person they expect to see in this building.

"How's your day going?" I ask them.

"Just fine," the woman says. "And yours?"

"Fine, ma'am."

The elevator arrives and the doors open. I wait, letting the elderly couple get on before I do. Then, when I get on and press the button for the top floor, they look at each other, the woman's eyes wide.

I take a look at the elevator pad. They live on the floor below Diana and me. Or they're going to visit someone there. It's Saturday morning, so it could be either.

When the elevator stops and opens on their floor, the woman smiles at me. "Have a wonderful day, young man."

"You too," I say as the doors close.

Her husband—I assume—looks back at me and frowns.

They don't see my type a whole lot here. Certainly not going to the penthouse.

With my luck, they'll probably call the cops on me the minute they're back in their place. Report the unsavory-looking guy with the long hair who's heading toward the apartment of the gorgeous woman living in the penthouse.

I huff out a breath. Despite all the bullshit I've gotten myself into over the years, I've never been arrested. Even when I should have been. Small mercies, I guess.

A moment later I'm knocking on Diana's door.

"Hey," she says as she opens the door. "You want some

help with those?"

"I got it." I walk in and head straight to the kitchen.

She crosses into the kitchen and opens the fridge. "You've got the bottom shelf in the refrigerator and on the door, for condiments. In the pantry, I gave you the high shelf since you're taller than I am."

"Got it."

I put my groceries away and then head back to my room. Now what?

I like to keep busy. Helps keep my head on straight. Keeps me from thinking about how much I want a drink or a hit.

And it keeps me from thinking about the horror of my childhood.

Keeps me from thinking about Griffin.

But the thing is, I've got nothing to do. When I was in rehab, there were all kinds of activities. I was able to keep my mind and body busy.

My body... I head back out of my room. Diana is still in the kitchen.

"So I was wondering," I say. "About the fitness center."

"What about it?"

"Am I able to use it?"

She cocks her head. "I don't see why not. You'll have to wait until you get your key. You'll need that to access it."

"Got it."

"Like I said, I'll go down to security and take care of it as soon as I can. Sometime today. But I've got someone coming at two."

"Oh?"

"Yeah. Just somebody from maintenance to do some work."

"I'm pretty handy. Maybe I can do it."

She looks away. "Don't be silly. That's what maintenance is for. They'll take care of it." She glances down at her phone sitting on the counter. "Looks like I've got time, so I'll go ahead down to security and take care of your keys."

"All right. I'll be here."

Diana nods and heads for the door.

I take a seat on the couch. It's in a gorgeous brown leather. Italian, maybe. I don't know a whole lot about leather. But I know it's got to be expensive.

Like this whole apartment that I'm staying in for free. Guilt gnaws at my throat.

I crane my head toward the door. "Diana?"

She turns around slowly. "Yes, Dragon?"

"What are you having done? I know you said you have a maintenance guy, but I'd like to do something to earn my keep if you won't take money."

She presses her lips together. "It's nothing too crazy. Just something for my bedroom door."

I cock my head. "You're having maintenance done on your door? What are they doing?"

She takes a deep breath in. "If you must know, I'm having a lock put on."

Something twists around my heart. I hang my head slightly. "Oh."

She takes a few steps into the apartment. "It's not that I think you're a bad guy, Dragon. Far from it. Brianna and Jesse think the world of you. It's just... I don't really know you."

She's silent for a moment. The awkwardness hangs in the air like a dead fish.

"I'm happy to ask them to put a lock on your door, too."

I shake my head. "No need. And I get it. You don't have to feel bad about putting a lock on the door. I'm sure I'd do the same thing."

"Right." She shifts her gaze around the room. "Well, anyway. See you later."

She walks toward the door.

I can't help but watch her. She's wearing black yoga pants and sneakers. A burgundy-colored sweatshirt with Steel Vineyards and their logo printed on it. Her long hair is pulled back into a high ponytail, and she's not wearing any makeup that I can tell.

She's still the most gorgeous creature I've ever laid eyes on.

I let myself stare since her back is to me.

But as she opens the door, she looks over her shoulder and meets my gaze. "For real, Dragon. The lock is just a precaution. Please don't read anything into it. I'll be back as soon as I can. Make yourself at home."

I nod, leaning back on the couch.

I will myself not to feel weird about Diana's lock.

If Griffin were still around, and she were staying with a man she hardly knew, I sure as hell would want her to have a lock on her door to keep him out at night.

Especially if...

I sigh.

Especially if it were a man like me.

CHAPTER SEVEN

DIANA

I don't drink.

I'm not an alcoholic, and I'm not a complete teetotaler. I'll drink a glass of sparkling wine on special occasions, but for the most part, I stay away from the stuff.

I stay away from it because of something that happened to me when I was a freshman in high school.

It was the homecoming bonfire, and I was the freshman attendant on the homecoming court. I was giddy about everything—about finally being in high school, about attending my first bonfire, but mostly about catching the eyes of the hunky football players.

The bonfires were known for the lethal punch they called Hairy Buffalo. It was in a big plastic garbage can, and it was supposed to be a bunch of fruit juices mixed together.

Of course, the scuttlebutt was that someone always spiked it, so I couldn't wait to try it.

That was a decision I would regret.

Not because of the alcohol in the punch—and it was a lot.

But mine was spiked with something else. I didn't find out what until I woke up in the hospital, lucky to be alive.

So I don't drink. I don't keep alcohol at my place.

And of course I don't do drugs.

Maybe that's why Brianna and Jesse were so adamant that Dragon stay with me.

Maybe they think I'll be a good influence on him.

But Dragon had maintained his sobriety for a while. In fact, according to Brianna, he even allowed himself to drink beer and smoke pot but stayed away from the hard stuff.

Until London, the night after the band's first performance... He blew it all.

Frankly, he shouldn't have been smoking pot or drinking beer. From what I understand about addicts, they have to stay away from all of it.

But Dragon thought he could handle it, and according to Jesse, he *did* handle it for many years.

What happened in London?

Was it simple fear of success? The band was finally making it big, so he tried to sabotage it?

None of my business. I can't concern myself with him. I've already made him feel weird about staying in my place now that he knows about the lock I'm installing.

No. He's lucky to be staying with me, and if he feels weird about the lock, that's not my problem. I need my head in the game with this new job. I'm so psyched about the project, and if I want to have my hands in it, I need to show the bosses right away that I'm serious about architecture and serious about their firm. Dragon's feelings are the least of my worries.

I make it down to security. "Hey," I say to Steve, the guard on duty.

"Ms. Steel. How can I help you?"

"I'm going to have someone staying at my place for a while, so I need to get him a couple of keys."

Steve nods. "Ronnie is in today. She can help you in the

office."

"Thanks, Steve."

He smiles. "Not a problem."

I walk behind the counter where Steve is sitting and then to the office where I knock on the open door, waving to Ronnie.

"Diana, can I help you?" Ronnie asks.

"Yeah," I say. "I have a...friend staying with me for a while. I need to get a couple of keys for him."

"Okay," she says. "I'm just going to need his name. I can give you a key for now, but have him stop by so I can get his ID."

"Absolutely. Sorry, I would've done that. I guess I didn't realize you needed it."

"We take security very seriously here. But don't worry. Just make sure he stops by in the next couple of days. In the meantime, I just need his name."

"It's Dragon. Dragon Locke. Lock with an e."

She raises her eyebrows. "You're kidding, right?"

"No, that's his name. You'll probably be hearing more about him. He's a member of a rock band that's on its way to making it big, I think."

"What's the name of the band?"

"Dragonlock."

"No, the name of the band."

I laugh. "They actually named the band after him. Dragonlock. All one word with no e on the end. But his name is Dragon, first name. Locke, last name."

She types on her computer. "If you say so." She laughs.

"He's the drummer. My brother-in-law, Jesse Pike, is one of the lead singers."

"Yeah, congratulations. I heard you just came back from a triple wedding."

"Quadruple, actually. My sister, Bree, and three of my cousins married four siblings from a neighboring ranch. It was a big affair."

"I'll bet." Ronnie shoves two keycards in her reader, digitally embedding them. Then she hands them to me. "These should get him everywhere he needs to go."

"Thank you." I grab the cards. "I'll tell him to come down as soon as he can to give you his ID."

"Great." She smiles wide. "Thanks, Diana. Enjoy your weekend."

"I will. It'll be my last free time for a while."

"Oh?"

"Yeah. I start a new job, my first as an associate architect, on Monday. I'm hoping to get assigned to a really big project, so I'll be working at least sixty hours a week. Maybe more."

"Don't forget to take some time for you, okay?"

"Thanks, I'll try." I give her a wave as I leave.

CHAPTER EIGHT

DRAGON

This last stint in rehab put me through a high-speed wash cycle and hung me out to dry.

I don't like to think about my past. I don't talk about it to anyone. Even Jesse doesn't know everything, and there are a few things that are such a blur, I'm not even sure exactly what happened.

But for the most part, it's out on the table now.

All starting with Griffin's birth. That pretty baby my parents brought home.

Everyone doted on her. Within two months, she had morphed into the most beautiful thing any of us had ever seen. Bright-blue eyes, a fuzzy bald head that was starting to sprout cotton-candy blond hair. Chubby red cheeks, full pink lips, and a toothless smile that melted my heart.

She smiled the most for me.

Even my mother noticed that. "Look at that, Felix. I'm the one who carried that child inside me for nine months, had terrible morning sickness and high blood pressure, and she only smiles for him."

"It's not a reflection on you, Stevie," Dad would say. "She just loves her big brother, and he loves her. Is that such a bad thing?"

Mom would sulk for a few minutes, but then it would be time to nurse Griffin, and she'd get the alone time she wanted with her daughter.

That was when Dad and I had our time. It was my father who gave me my first drum. The memory collides into my mind, and though I try to stop it, it unfolds in technicolor inside my head.

"Son, I got a bonus at work the other day. I brought you a present."

I jump up and down, clapping my hands. "I love presents!"

"I know you do, Dragon, and we don't have a lot of money for presents, but with Griffin arriving, and her getting all the attention, I thought you might like something for yourself."

He presents me with a large box wrapped in paper with dragons printed on it.

I rip the paper off, open the box, and inside—

"Oh, wow! A drum!"

Dad smiles warmly. "Yes, it's a drum, Dragon. When you were a little boy, still in your highchair, you used to bang your hands on the tray, and I swear to God, I heard rhythm in your creations. I said to your mother, 'Stevie, that boy is going to be a drummer.'"

Dad pulls the drum out of the box and sets it in front of me.

I start beating it with my fists. Bang, bang, bang. Thud, thud, thud.

"You use these." Dad hands me two wooden sticks.

I take each of them in a fist and bang on the drum. This time it clicks, like a snapping sound. I like it.

Dad smiles. "You'll get the hang of it. You're young yet, but someday I think you're going to be a mighty fine drummer."

I don't care about being a drummer. All I care about is that I got a present. My daddy bought me a present, and it makes me feel good. All warm inside. Because ever since Griffin was born, she seems to get all the presents. Mom and Dad say that's what happens when you bring a new baby into the house, and that I got just as many presents when I was born. I don't remember any of that, though, so I'm not sure I believe it.

My new drum is red and shiny. The top is white and shiny, and the lines on the sides are silver.

"It's called a snare drum, Dragon."

"Snare drum," I growl. "Sounds like a snarl."

"Kind of," Dad says, "but the drum has nothing to do with snarling. The snare drum is a central piece in a drum set."

"Drum set?"

"Yeah. That's a collection of different drums and other things that are used in lots of music. But the snare drum is the best drum to learn the basic rhythms on, especially at your age."

I beat on the drum with the sticks, enjoying the sharp sound.

Dad crouches down and looks into my eyes. "You have to take care of your drum, Dragon. This is an actual musical instrument, and I know you're young, but I want you to have it."

"Thanks, Daddy." I continue beating on the drum.

"Dragon."

I look up, still playing.

He grabs my hands mid-beat. "I'm serious. This isn't just a toy. I want you to have fun with it, but it's an actual musical instrument that you need to take care of. Now, I'm going to help you because you're so young. I'll show you how to take care of it, and then, as you get older, I'm going to expect you to do it."

I nod vigorously. "Okay, Daddy. I promise I'll take good care of it."

"And there's one other thing," Dad says.

"What's that?"

"You can only play it in the garage."

I frown. "Why, Daddy?"

"Because we have a new baby in the house. The drum might wake up Griffin. She needs her sleep, and so does your mom."

I frown again.

"No frowning, son. I know how much you love your little sister."

Then I smile. "I do. I love her so much."

"Then you need to do what's good for her as well. So we're going to put your drum in the garage, and you'll have certain times when you can go out and play it."

"Okay, Daddy." I smile again.

Because the first time I laid eyes on that little baby, I knew I would do anything for her.

Even if it means playing my drum in the garage.

It didn't take me long to unpack. I stay in the bedroom Diana assigned. It feels weird to leave, walk around a place that isn't mine. Part of me feels like I'm back in my room in rehab, not sure what to do next.

Except I don't have activities or therapy to go to during the day. They keep us on a strict schedule in rehab to keep our minds busy so we won't think about drugs or alcohol.

Of course, all we think about is drugs and alcohol.

That's the life of an addict. It's always there in the back of my mind. I can leave it there, but I'll never forget about it. It's like a shadow lurking in a dark alley, ready to resurface at the slightest provocation.

Luckily, I'm not easily provoked. But it's still there, haunting me, sometimes even jeering at me.

What also jeers at me is the fact that Jesse and Brianna helped pay for my rehab stay. They said I didn't have to pay them back, but I will. Somehow I'll find a way.

I stayed there for six months. It didn't take long for me to dry out, but I stayed because I needed to take it seriously this time. I couldn't be half-assed about it like I was last time. No more pot and no more booze.

An addict is an addict, and you can't allow yourself gateway drugs and still expect to stay sober.

I did it for several years, and I honestly thought I had it figured out.

Until that night in London, after the concert.

The two women, both brunettes—I have no idea what their names are, and I don't rightfully care—push me down on the bed and then strip their clothes off.

Their tits are pert and bouncy, and I've got one huge-assed hard-on.

I'm still high on adrenaline from the concert. Man, we rocked it. All the Emerald Phoenix fans loved us, and lots of groupies stuck around us after the show—including these two.

Jesse took off, so I'm alone in the room with these ladies.

"You got anything to drink in here?" one of them asks in her British accent.

"Should be something in the minifridge," I say.

She saunters over to the minifridge, opens it, and pulls out some cans of some kind of ale. "This what you mean?"

"Yeah. Help yourself. If we run out, we can have some sent up."

She takes a can of beer, pops the tab open, and hands it to her friend. Then she pops another one and takes a long drink.

"You want one?" she asks me.

"Sure. Bring it on over."

She pops the third can and sets it on the nightstand next to the bed. "So you up for some fun?"

"I figured that's why we're here," I say in a slow drawl, which sounds so different from their flirty English accents.

"Then let's start with getting you undressed." Lady one climbs on top of me, pulls me into a sitting position, and then she slides my black T-shirt over my head.

She drops her jaw. "God, you're sexy. Nipple rings."

Lady two flicks them, licking her lips. "Fuck, yes, they're sexy. Do they hurt?"

I shake my head.

"Good." She leans down and slides her lips over one of them.

My nipples are more sensitive than the average man's, and boy, does that get me going.

"What a great tattoo." Lady one traces her fingers over the dragon that covers a large portion of my chest.

I only have one other tattoo   on the back of my thigh, where I can't see it.

I have my reasons for having the tattoo, and also for not wanting to see it.

"Let's get those fucking pants off you," Lady two says. She unties my black boots and slides them off my feet along with my *socks.*

Lady one works on my belt and zipper and then my black jeans. "God, you're fucking sexy," she says.

"So are you."

Once my jeans are off and my cock is free, they both widen their eyes at my girth. Yeah, I'm not just long. I'm thick. I've had women run away screaming.

But not these two. They want to fuck a rock star.

I'm far from a rock star. I'm Emerald Phoenix's sloppy seconds, but who the fuck cares? I'm going to get laid by two hotties, and boy, am I ready.

CHAPTER NINE

DIANA

I return, and Dragon's door is shut.

I knock. "Dragon?"

He opens the door. He's changed clothes, and he's wearing jeans and a black-and-white striped button-down.

He looks...

Damned good.

"Got your keys." I pull them out of my pocket. "You get two in case you lose one. They'll get you into the building, into the penthouse, and into the fitness room."

"Thanks." He takes them, pulls a wallet out of his pocket, and shoves them inside.

I widen my eyes at the "thanks." Is it the first one I've actually gotten?

I still feel like I'm on thin ice after the awkward conversation about the lock on my door, so I'll take it. I give him a weak smile and turn away when the low rumble of his voice sends another chill up my spine.

I grab my phone. "We should exchange cell phone numbers too, since we'll be living together and all."

He grabs his phone. "Sure. Good idea."

We quickly exchange information, and he shoves his phone back into his pocket.

"So...I was thinking..." he begins.

I turn around. "What?"

"I'd like to take you out to dinner." A small burst of pink rushes onto his cheek. "You know, in appreciation for what you're doing for me."

I cock my head. Is he serious? Does he really think one dinner is going to pay for a room in my penthouse?

But when I look into his eyes, I see something there. He wants to do this. Perhaps it's all he *can* do.

"That's not necessary," I say.

"I know." He shoves his hands into his pockets. "If you want to turn me down, I totally get it. I brought in groceries. I can make myself a sandwich. But I'd like to do this, and believe me, I won't be asking you again. Not until I get a steady stream of income coming in."

He looks sincere, and damn, his eyes are beautiful.

Every time I talk to him—which has only been a few times back at my parents' home on the western slope when the band's played at their parties—I can't help but notice his eyes. So magnificent and breathtaking but always laced with a bit of sadness. As if there's something inside him that he doesn't talk about, doesn't even think about. Yet it's always there, an undertone in everything else he is.

I smile. This time it's not so forced. "Okay. Where do you want to go?"

"There's this great little diner a couple of blocks down. I went there sometimes during rehab." He presses his lips together. "Once I was allowed to leave, that is. I know it's not what you're used to, but—"

I hold up a hand to stop him. "That sounds lovely. When do you want to leave?"

He pulls his phone out of his pocket. "It's five o'clock. Now would be a good time since it's Saturday night. We'll probably beat the crowds."

"All right. Let me change."

"You don't need to change. You look great."

"I'm in sweats." I let out a soft chuckle. "I'll change."

He frowns and looks down at the shirt he's wearing. "You want me to change?"

"God, no. You look great. I'm just going to throw on some jeans and a nicer shirt. I won't be but a minute."

I leave him standing there and walk to my master bedroom.

It's about twice the size of Dragon's room. I feel like I should have given him the larger second bedroom.

But he seems fine. He even seems grateful, though he has trouble saying it. Buying me dinner will probably take all the spare cash he has, which is part of the reason why I didn't want him to do it. The other part is that it's going to be so awkward.

But it seems important to him, and I do want to help. Brianna thinks this is where he should be, and though part of me believes that's due to her being a little dick-whipped and wanting to do anything for her new husband, another part knows my sister. She's young and vivacious and a little full of herself sometimes, but she's also a genuinely kind person.

I head into my walk-in closet, grab a pair of straight-leg jeans and, instead of a blouse, I choose a V-neck sweater. It's October, and the weather is a bit brisk today. I throw some suede booties on my feet, grab a light jacket, and I'm ready to go.

I walk out, head to Dragon's door, but then hear his voice. "I'm over here."

He's in the large living area, sitting on my leather couch.

Again, I'm struck by how good he looks. What a handsome man he is, even with his long hair.

He took it out of its band, and it's floating around his shoulders in stark contrast to the white stripes on his shirt.

"Don't you want to wear a jacket?" I ask.

"I was good when I went out to the market earlier."

"Okay, if you say so. But it's a little brisk."

"I'll be fine."

We don't say anything else as we leave the penthouse and descend in the elevator. When we walk past security, I grab his arm. "I forgot to tell you. I need you to stop at security and show them your ID."

"What for?"

"They need the information for you to stay here. To give you a key."

He furrows his brow. "You already gave me a key."

"I know, but they gave it to me on the condition that you come down and show your ID."

"You want me to do it now?"

"No. It's after five on a Saturday, so the office manager is gone. You'll need to do it Monday, okay?"

"Yeah, sure. Whatever."

Great. Now he's going to think that I don't trust him again. That I want his ID on file in case he robs me blind or something. But this is the building's policy, not mine. And the lock on my door is just common sense...

Whatever. I'm not going to think about it. He's lucky to be staying with me, so I really shouldn't sweat the minutiae of his every feeling. If I had taken any other guy I barely knew in, I wouldn't be worrying about how he reacted to my every move.

Why do I care with Dragon?

I shake the thoughts out of my head. He's taking me to dinner, which means he at least wants to demonstrate his gratitude. I won't worry anymore.

We leave the building, and I wave to Steve, who's still on duty.

"That your new housemate?" he asks.

"Yeah." I motion Dragon over. "This is Dragon Locke. Dragon, this is Steve. One of our security officers."

"Good to meet you." Steve holds out his hand.

Dragon shakes it. "Yeah, you too."

"Usually takes me a few days to remember names of our new residents, but I don't think Dragon is one I'll forget." Steve lets out a chuckle.

Dragon doesn't react. I'd bet he's heard that joke hundreds of times.

"That's what it says on my birth certificate," Dragon drawls as he heads to the door.

I give Steve a weak and apologetic smile and follow Dragon out the door.

The diner, which is aptly called the Rocky Mountain Diner, is about a block and half down, and I'm oddly touched when, as we start walking, Dragon moves himself to my other side, blocking me from the street. I'm used to being treated like a lady. All the men in my family have been brought up to be gentlemen. But admittedly, I didn't expect such chivalrous behavior from Dragon.

We get to the diner, and he also opens the door for me.

"Thank you," I murmur.

The diner is already full, so we head to the host's stand. "Hi, how long for a table for two?" I ask.

He glances down. "Looks like it's going to be about twenty-five to thirty minutes. Is that okay?" Then he spies Dragon behind me. "Hey, dude. Where you been?"

"Back on the western slope for a few weeks. Had a wedding to attend."

"Great to have you back. You want your usual table?"

"Sure, if it's open."

The host—his nametag says Tex, of all things—glances around toward the back of the diner. "Looks like Lexi's cleaning it right now. I'll get you two seated in a minute."

"Wait a minute," I say. "You just told me half an hour."

"That's before I knew you were with Dragon here." He nods in Dragon's direction, smiling. "He's a regular. We always have a table for him."

I widen my eyes and look at Dragon.

He simply shrugs.

A few minutes later, Tex leads us back around the corner to a tiny booth. "You can see why this place is always available," Tex says to me. "Sometimes we don't even use it—only when we're incredibly busy like tonight."

The booth indeed has seen better days. The plastic coating on the table is cracked, and the vinyl covering the two benches is ripped. It's smaller too—a booth for two as opposed to the other booths that seat four or six.

"Have you been here before?" Tex asks me.

"Afraid I haven't. But I'm looking forward to it."

He gestures to the napkin holder against the wall. "Menus are in there. And the Saturday night special is Salisbury steak with mashed potatoes and green beans."

"Sounds good, Tex," Dragon says. "Obliged."

Tex nods. "Glad to see you back, Dragon. Hope to see you

around." He heads back to the host's stand.

"Hey, Dragon." A blond waitress approaches us. "Tex said you were back."

"Hey, Lexi," Dragon says. "This is Diana."

Lexi smiles sweetly at me. "Good to meet you, Diana. Did Tex tell you about tonight's special?"

"Salisbury steak with mashies," Dragon says. "Sounds good to me."

I can't help but smile. Dragon, the brooding rock star, just referred to mashed potatoes as mashies. In public, in front of a perfect stranger.

Underneath his gloomy exterior, could there be something light, even playful?

"Tex probably neglected to mention that our special tonight is also cherry pie." She winks at Dragon. "And I *know* you love cherry pie." She turns to me. "What can I get for you, doll?"

"Uh...I haven't looked at the menu yet." At the moment, I'm too busy wondering why Dragon told me he didn't like sweets when he obviously loves cherry pie. "Can I have a minute?"

"You sure can. I'll be back in a flash." She rushes away.

"I always get the special when I come here," Dragon says. "They sell a lot of it, so it's always hot and fresh."

Does that mean the other food is not hot and fresh? Salisbury steak doesn't sound great to me. I'm kind of a beef snob. You can't grow up on a beef ranch and not be, so when I'm out, and it's a place that doesn't source its beef from my family's ranch, I usually get chicken or fish.

I grab a menu and open it. A blob of ketchup greets me. I take a napkin and wipe it off.

"I guess I'll have..." I scan the menu. "You have any recommendations?"

"Like I said, I almost always get the special. But I hear the chicken fingers are okay."

I glance down. Chicken fingers served with fries and a side of coleslaw. That'll work. "Chicken fingers it is." I close my menu and return it to the holder.

Lexi returns with two glasses of water and sets them down. "You decided yet, doll?"

"Yes, upon recommendation, I will have the chicken fingers, please."

"Good choice. And you, the special." She makes notes on her pad and then shoves it in her apron pocket. "Shouldn't be too long."

She whisks away, and to have something to do, I pick up my glass of water and take a drink.

Then I look around the diner. Despite the fact that our tiny booth in the back corner has seen better days, the rest of the place is kind of charming. I almost feel like I've been transported back a few decades.

"How come this is your table?" I ask Dragon.

He shrugs. "Because it's usually available, and I like it. Seems to fit me."

"The other booths are bigger and nicer," I say.

"I know, but I usually dine alone, so why should I take up more space than I need?"

I suppose he has a point there.

"Besides, I like this booth," he continues. "It's cozy. Sometimes I play a game on my phone. Other times, when I remember to, I bring a book to read."

Again, Dragon surprises me. I wouldn't take him for the

type who would be reading a book alone in a diner.

I lean toward him. "What do you like to read?"

He twitches his nose. "It's a little outdated, but I've been working my way through the works of Charles Dickens. I just rounded off *Great Expectations.*"

I widen my eyes. A meteor could strike this diner, and that would be less shocking to me. Dragon has an unmistakable darkness about him, but he's got a playful side *and* a well-read side. I'm intrigued as all get-out.

"You there, Diana?"

I nod, take a drink of water. "Yeah, I just didn't take you for the Dickens type, I suppose."

He frowns. "You pegged me more as the trash TV type?"

"No, no," I sputter. "I just... I wish I had more time to read the classics. Or at least the initiative to get through them. I'm impressed, that's all."

Dragon exhales sharply. "Well, I don't always read when I'm here. Sometimes I just like to sit in the booth and think."

"About what?"

"Personal stuff." He looks down at the table.

Message received. He's not going to tell me.

Not that I can blame him. He and I don't know each other very well yet.

We may never know each other well.

I think back to the conversation I had with him at one of my mother's infamous parties at our ranch house. It was a couple of weeks before Christmas, after Dragonlock had played at a local concert at the cinema with a special guest appearance by Emerald Phoenix.

I was standing alone near the pool house, and Dragon—to my surprise—approached me.

—•

"How are you doing tonight, Diana?" Dragon asks me.

"Great, how are you?"

He nods slowly. "Good. You enjoy the concert?"

"Absolutely. All of it. Even Rory's operatic numbers."

"I guess this is her opera swan song," Dragon says.

"So I've heard. She's going for rock and roll."

"And she can rock."

I nod. I'm feeling a little awkward. Dragon holds a beer, and I have a flute full of champagne.

He gestures to the flute. "You like that stuff?"

"Yeah. It's good. My uncle Ryan does a great job with the sparkling wines. But honestly, I don't drink much."

"Really?" He wrinkles his forehead.

"Does that surprise you?"

He cocks his head. "Well...yeah. You're a member of the Steel family. They all drink. A lot."

I raise an eyebrow. "Excuse me?"

"I'm not saying they're drunks or anything, but look around you." He gestures to a few nearby members of my family, who are indeed imbibing. "The alcohol is flowing."

I can't fault his observation. My family enjoys the finer things in life, and that includes good booze. "Yeah. My dad loves his bourbon, and my brother Dale loves his wine. Then there's Donny." I can't help a giggle.

"What about him?"

"He likes sweet drinks. His favorite is a margarita."

That gets a low chuckle out of Dragon. "He doesn't look like the margarita type."

"I know. But he loves them. Drives Dad and Dale crazy.

Especially Dale, since he appreciates all the nuances of the wine he makes."

"Funny." Dragon takes a sip of his beer. Then, "Well, nice to see you." He saunters off.

And I'm left to think about what an enigma he is. First, his name. That in itself is interesting. Second, he's so quiet. And there's a definite darkness about him—a darkness that, quite frankly, is very intriguing. Attractive, even.

Then those eyes...

Even under the artificial torchlight in our backyard, they glitter with gold flecks.

I finish my champagne and set my empty flute on one of the trays available for the bartenders to take care of.

And then I don't think about Dragon again.

CHAPTER TEN

DRAGON

Diana's quiet, but it doesn't bother me.

I'm used to quiet.

I like it.

I'm not a big talker myself, especially when people ask me about my past. Or even about my present. Come to think of it, I'm not too keen to discuss the future, either.

During this last rehab, though, I went into some in-depth therapy. It took some time. For the first few sessions, I didn't say a damned word.

Then I finally realized that Jesse and Brianna were paying for this, so I'd better make the most of it. I owed Jess that much after what I put him through in Europe.

So I opened up, and once I did, the choice was no longer mine.

The memories had to get out because what was inside was eating me alive.

I told that therapist things I had never said aloud.

Things I hadn't even let myself think about for so long.

Even so... I still kept one big secret to myself.

That one... I don't think I'll ever let out.

My thoughts are interrupted when Lexi comes back with our food.

Diana's chicken fingers look pretty darned good, and the fries look fresh and crispy.

In opposition, my Salisbury steak looks a little gray around the gills. It smells okay—beefy and savory—but I'm thinking about what Diana's crispy fries might feel like as I bite into them.

Not a problem, though. The special is always cheap, and I'm used to industrial-type food. It's pretty much all we got at rehab.

"Thank you." Diana smiles at Lexi.

"Not a problem, sweetheart. You two just let me know if you need anything else, okay?" Lexi flaunts away.

Diana inhales and then grabs a napkin from the holder and places it in her lap. Is she waiting for me to eat?

"Please, go ahead."

She smiles, picks up her knife and fork, and cuts a piece off one of her chicken fingers.

Seriously? She's eating chicken fingers with a knife and fork? It's a little ridiculous, but also just a touch endearing. She's so well-mannered.

That said, if she does the same with her fries, I may have to say something.

She doesn't though, thank God. She grabs the bottle of ketchup from the holder and squeezes some onto her plate. Then she picks up a fry, dips it, and takes a bite.

I actually hear the crispy crunch when she bites into it.

And I'm really wanting a fry.

"You want to try a fry?" she asks.

"That's okay."

"You sure? Because you're eyeing them like a dog salivating over a Thanksgiving turkey."

I avert my gaze. "No, I'm not."

She lets out a low chuckle. "Actually, you are." She picks up a fry. "Ketchup?"

I nod.

She swirls it in the ketchup and then hands it to me.

I take it from her—it would be rude not to—and bite off half of the fry. The tomato tang of the ketchup and the warm crispiness of the potato... I close my eyes. Man, I do love fries. I savor it, and then I try the Salisbury steak.

The flavor is decent. Basic. I like basic. Basic doesn't judge you. It just is.

I know what good food is. I've been to enough parties at Diana's parents' house. They put together massive galas, and they often hire Dragonlock to perform. The other band members and I get to partake in whatever huge feast they put out for the night.

Steel beef is usually a centerpiece—grass-fed meat that melts in your mouth. One of Diana's aunts is a gourmet chef, so the spread is always spectacular.

So is the drink—usually wine paired with the food and provided by Steel Vineyards.

I sigh.

I won't be tasting any of that wine anymore.

No more pot either.

My counselors at the rehab center were amazed that I'd been able to go so long with the gateway substances of beer, wine, and marijuana.

Those days are over.

Diana takes another bite of her chicken, bringing the breaded meat between her full pink lips.

And all I can think about is how lucky that piece of chicken finger is.

I desperately want to ask her for another fry, but I don't. They're her fries. Sure, I'm paying for them, but I'm staying at her place for free. I get my own fully furnished room plus access to all the amenities of her building.

So the fact that I bought her chicken fingers and fries?

It means shit.

We don't talk a lot, but Diana seems comfortable with that. She's a lot quieter than her sister, Brianna. Brianna likes to talk, laugh, flirt, be the life of the party.

Now that she's married to Jesse, will she still be like that?

Probably. Tigers don't change their stripes just because they enter into holy matrimony.

At least that's what I figure. Not that I'd know.

I've cleaned my plate, and once Diana has finished her last bite of chicken fingers, Lexi arrives.

"How was everything?" she asks.

"Lovely, thank you." Diana gives Lexi that beautiful smile.

"And you, Dragon?"

"As ever, Lexi."

"Good enough." She clears our plates, and less than a minute later, she returns with two servings of cherry pie.

"On the house for you and your special lady, Dragon." She slides the plates in front of each of us. "I know cherry's your favorite."

My cheeks warm at her use of the words *special lady*, and I can tell Diana's are too, because they turn a gorgeous shade of rose.

"Oh"—I clear my throat—"we're not..."

Lexi widens her eyes. "I'm sorry. I didn't mean to assume anything. I hope you enjoy the pie." Lexi's cheeks are pink as she leaves.

Diana breaks the silence after what feels like an eternity. "It's very kind of you," she says. "I'm sure it will be delicious."

I look down at my pie, avoiding Diana's gaze. "Sorry about that."

"That's no problem. But I have a question."

"Yeah?"

She cuts off a bite of pie with her fork and brings it to her lips, holding it there in midair. "You told me you weren't much for sweets. But Lexi said cherry pie is your favorite."

Fuck. Did I say that? Yeah, I did, when she offered me ice cream. I don't know why the hell I say half the things I do.

Except that's a damned lie. I said it because she'd already fed me and I didn't feel comfortable taking more of her food, even though I was taking my own sweet time with those last few potato chips so I wouldn't have to leave.

Just a few more minutes to be near her. In her presence. In her light.

"I might have fibbed a little," I finally say.

She raises her eyebrows as she takes the bite of pie into her mouth.

"I guess I just didn't want to bother you anymore last night. But in truth, I love dessert."

She nods as she chews. She'll no doubt interrogate me once she swallows.

But instead, she widens her eyes. "Wow! That's some of the most delicious pie I've ever eaten. And Aunt Marjorie makes amazing pies."

"They make them all fresh here," I say. "Using lard for the crust. The old-fashioned way."

She takes another bite, this time chewing a bit more

slowly. "Yeah, I can tell there's something different about the crust. But it's not just the crust. It's the filling, too. This isn't cherry pie filling out of a can. It's got a certain tartness to it, and it's delicious."

I'm not sure what to say to that. I would assume Diana knows what she's talking about since her family is so into food. I wouldn't know the difference between filling out of a can and homemade filling. But the diner's pies are to die for, and Lexi's right. Cherry is my favorite.

My mom's cherry pies are one of my few fond memories of my childhood. It was Griffin's favorite too.

But I wipe the thought from my mind.

I can't go down that avenue. Not in Diana Steel's company. She's a bright and sparkling light, and just being with her makes my own dark soul a little easier to deal with.

I finish my pie just as Diana is taking her last bite.

"That was absolutely delicious. Crazy that a pie at this little hole in the wall in Denver is better than my aunt's." Then she clamps her hand over her mouth. "Oh my God. I didn't mean to imply—"

"Don't apologize." I gesture around the small diner. "This is a hole in the wall. It's a dive. But I like it."

She smiles at me then, and it's a warm and genuine smile. "You know what, Dragon? I like it too."

CHAPTER ELEVEN

DIANA

Silence between us doesn't seem so awkward. Once we're back at the penthouse, Dragon goes to his room.

Fine with me. It saves me from having to make conversation.

Seems a waste of my last Saturday night before I'll be working my ass off, but really, what else is there to do?

I could call some friends. Maybe go out to a club.

My friend Teddy Holmes is an executive assistant at the architecture firm where I did my internship. She's always up for a good time, although she probably already has plans.

Still, what the hell? I grab my phone from the counter where I set it when we got home, and I'm about to call her when it buzzes.

It's Brianna.

"What's up, Bree?" I say into the phone. "Aren't you supposed to be humping your new husband on your honeymoon?"

"Don't be so gross," she says. "Jesse's in the shower, and I wanted to give you a call. Thank you again for what you're doing for Dragon."

"Consider it my good deed for the week."

"How's everything going?"

"He just moved in today, Bree." I glance toward the door to Dragon's room. It's closed, probably locked. "But it's fine. Once I start work, I'm not going to be here for more than sleeping, so we certainly won't get in each other's way."

"Thanks for doing this," she says again. "It means so much to Jesse and to me."

"You don't have to keep thanking me. I'm glad to do it." Maybe not glad exactly, but it's not imposing on my life that much. "What are you guys up to?"

"A lot of lying on the beach... A lot of sex..."

My little sister is having way more sex than I am, but oh well.

"How are you liking Jamaica?"

"Oh my God, loving it. The food is to die for, the beaches are gorgeous and serene, and the people... So friendly."

"I was surprised you and Jesse didn't decide to go back to Europe after you didn't get to finish the tour with them."

"We'll go to Europe eventually. But Jesse just spent several months there, and he totally needed a relaxing honeymoon. And Jamaica is so relaxing. Even the activities we've done— hiking up Dunn's River Falls and horseback riding on the beach—it's all been sublime."

I scowl at the thought of hiking on a vacation. "A *hike* was sublime?"

"Absolutely. You actually hike *up* the waterfall, but remember we're at sea level, Dee. Compared to living at elevation in Colorado, there's so much more oxygen in the air here, not to mention the oxygen pouring off from the water molecules... It's invigorating. An amazing experience."

"Sounds awesome. Maybe I'll get to Jamaica myself sometime soon."

"You totally should. That's where your next vacation should be."

I laugh out loud. "I'm not going to have a vacation for a while, Bree. This new job is going to keep me on my toes. I have to prove my worth if I want to get on that mountaintop project."

"You will. You're the best they've got."

I smile into the phone. My little sister and I have always gotten along pretty well. We're four years apart and different as night and day. At her age, she can keep her svelte body without even thinking about dieting. Now that I'm inching toward my late twenties, the same can't be said about me.

Of course, Brianna also runs ten miles a day and works a lot of calories off outside in our family's orchards. She's a cowgirl all the way, whereas I'm more comfortable in an urban setting, despite how I grew up.

"I'll let you go," Brianna says. "Thanks again, and don't hesitate to call if you need anything."

I chuckle. "You're kidding, right? You really want to give me carte blanche to call you while you're on your honeymoon?"

She giggles into the phone. "You know what I mean. If you need anything or have questions about Dragon or whatever. Jesse's the guy to ask. He knows Dragon better than anyone."

I look back at Dragon's door and frown. "I get the feeling that no one really knows Dragon."

"You may be right," she says. "Jesse has kind of alluded to that, though he's pretty sure he knows Dragon better than anyone else does. Besides Dragon...maybe."

"Jesse and his therapist at rehab, I guess," I say. "Have a great time, Bree. Soak up that sun and as much relaxation as you can. I'm a bit envious."

"Are you kidding? You're going to love this new job, Dee. You've always been happier when you're working."

"You're not wrong."

"Nope, I'm not. Keep Jesse and me posted, okay?"

"I will."

"Bye."

"Bye." I end the call.

Then I punch in Teddy's number. It's still early, so even if she does have plans, she may still be home.

"Dee!" she shouts into the phone.

Murmurs of voices permeate the line.

"Hey, I just wanted to check and see if you had plans for tonight. I want to go out."

"You're not going to believe this," she says. "There's an impromptu party going on at my place. I swear to God, I didn't plan it, or of course I would've invited you. But please, come on over."

"What?"

"Yeah. Seriously. A couple of friends from out of town popped in to say hi, and they brought a bunch of booze and some really good pot. I know you don't drink much and you don't smoke at all, but we've got some music playing, and my cousin and a couple of my neighbors stopped by. Come on over."

"Okay." I check the time on my phone. "This is my last night to party before I start a new job, so yeah, I'll be there. I just need to change."

"Awesome. See you in a few."

Teddy lives in a loft a couple of blocks away from my building, and her place has a great rooftop for parties. I imagine that's where we'll end up if the weather holds.

I love a good party. Even though I don't drink and I'm more the quiet type, I love music and good conversation.

I love the big city and everything it offers. Granted, Denver is not as huge as Chicago, New York, or LA, but I love it. It's home.

I head to my bedroom and take a look at myself in my full-length mirror.

I decide not to change after all. What I'm wearing is good enough for an impromptu party. Jeans and my sweater. I let my hair down out of its ponytail, and it falls over my shoulders. I also apply a little bit of makeup—just some lipstick, blush, and mascara. Once I'm satisfied, I leave the master bedroom.

To my surprise, Dragon is sitting in the living area reading something on his phone.

"Oh, hi," I say. "I'm going out for the evening."

His gaze stays fixed on his phone. "Okay."

"This is my last night to party before I start that new job, which may be taking all my waking hours."

Why am I explaining myself to him? I'm an adult, as is he. We're allowed to have our own lives.

He doesn't look up. "Got it."

Invite him to come with you, a little voice says inside my head.

No.

"Anyway, I'll see you."

I walk toward the door, grabbing my purse and phone on the way, and then take my leather jacket from the coat rack. I'm ready to leave when something seems to take over my body as I look over my shoulder.

"You want to come along?" I ask.

"What?" Dragon looks up from his phone.

"It's just a casual party over at my friend's house." I frown. "Well, not house so much as a loft. It's a couple of blocks from here. Some friends of hers came in from... Oh, never mind."

"Never mind?"

"I'm so sorry." My cheeks warm. "Teddy—that's my friend—mentioned that some friends came in from out of town and they brought a lot of booze and pot." I cross my arms, feeling blood rush through them. "So, yeah. I am so, so sorry that I wasn't thinking. I should never have invited you to go."

He rises then, his forehead wrinkled. "You don't think I can handle it?"

"No. I just mean..." I twist a lock of hair around my finger, embarrassment surging through me. "I don't know what I mean."

"Part of recovery is being able to resist," he says. "It might be good for me to be around that stuff."

"You're staying in Denver because you want to be close to rehab, right?"

"Yeah. In case I relapse. But I can't stop living life, Diana. I'm going to be around drugs and alcohol. I have to deal. You do, don't you?"

"I don't touch pot," I say. "I really hate it, to be honest. I have a drink or two, but not much."

"Yet you can be around people who are getting shit-faced."

"Well, yeah, but I'm not..."

"Not an addict?"

God, have I dug myself a giant hole.

I take a deep breath. "No. I mean, I hate to be so blunt, Dragon, but I'm not an addict."

"And I am."

"Well... Yeah. I don't think that's ever been an issue."

IAM SIN

He raises a hand in front of him. "I don't mean it that way. I am an addict. It's part of who I am. I can't escape it no matter how I try, but I can control it. I can't change who I am, but I can change how I deal with it. Just like I can't change my past." He stops abruptly.

And I can't help myself. "Is there something you wish you could change?"

"I don't talk about that," he says. "My point is only that there are some things I can't change. There is no point in trying because it would be fruitless. But what I can change is my attitude, my behavior. Maybe going out tonight—being around the stuff I need to avoid—would be a good test for me."

"You were around booze at the wedding."

"I was, but I also had all my friends around me then as well. Jesse was there, looking after me."

"And you don't think I would be looking after you?"

"Why would you? It's not like we're friends, Diana."

His words strike me with something I'm not prepared for.

He's right, of course. We're not friends. We had all of one or two conversations—short ones at that—before he moved in with me.

We're not friends. We're roommates. That's it.

I'm not sure how to respond to his comment, though, so I simply say, "Are you coming or not?"

"Sure. Let me get my jacket."

The doorman at Teddy's building knows me, and he waves us through. Once we get to her loft, I knock loudly, as I can already hear the music blaring.

Teddy answers the door clad in black skinny jeans and a peach camisole. She looks amazing, of course, her flaming red hair always a showstopper.

"Dee!" She grabs me into a hug. She breaks the embrace with wide eyes. "And who's this?"

"This is my new...roommate. Dragon."

"No*t the* Dragon." Teddy's eyes widen. "From the band?"

"One and the same," Dragon says.

Her jaw drops. "Oh my God! I can't believe it! Come on in, both of you. This is quite a treat." Teddy takes Dragon's arm and pulls him inside.

Teddy's loft isn't huge, which is why her parties often end up on the roof. But although the music is loud, only about eight people are here.

"Let me introduce you guys to everybody." Teddy turns to a man standing by her stereo. "Turn down the music, will you, Bud?"

Once the music goes down and we can hear ourselves think, Teddy grabs Dragon. "Most of you guys know Diana," she says, "except for Bud and Tracy. This is my great friend Diana Steel. But this is so exciting. Not that you aren't exciting, Dee, but we have a bona fide rock star here!"

Everyone gushes.

"This is Dragon. *The* Dragon of Dragonlock."

"The drummer?" a young woman dressed in shorts—yes, shorts and fishnet hose   asks.

She must be Tracy, since I don't recognize her.

"Yeah," Teddy says. "The band that opened for Emerald Phoenix on their European tour earlier this year."

Except Dragon wasn't there. He was at one concert before he came home and went into rehab. He's not correcting her, though, so I figure it's not my place to do it either.

Tracy—or so I assume—flits over to him. "Can I get you anything? A drink?"

"Just water," Dragon says in his low voice.

"But I brought this delicious craft IPA. You've got to try it."

"No, thank you."

"Pretty please?" She turns her lips into a flirty pout.

I'm about to open my mouth to tell her to shut up, that he's an addict, but he actually gives her a smile.

It's a small smile, but it's a smile. More than he's ever given me.

"I'm an addict," he says. "So no, thank you."

She drops her jaw. "Oh my God, I'm so sorry."

"You didn't know." That's all he says.

She's still holding on to his arm. "Let's get you that water, and then I want to talk to you all about your career."

I sigh and turn to Teddy. "Guess I don't have to worry about him having a good time."

"Tracy's such a groupie. I doubt she even knows much about Dragonlock. She'll screw anything that even slightly exudes rock and roll."

"Oh?"

"Oh, yeah." She smirks. "I mean, she's one of my closest friends, but she's a total...you know. We went to college together."

"So she and Bud aren't together?"

Teddy cracks a sly smile and narrows her eyes. "Depends on what you mean by together. They're friends with benefits, but they both screw whoever they want. Sometimes together."

I try to cover my surprise.

But Teddy just laughs. "You're such an innocent, Diana."

"Growing up on a secluded ranch on the western slope will do that."

Except I'm not an innocent. Maybe when it comes to things like sex. And that, you know, I like it to be with one other person max.

The thought of Dragon getting naked with Tracy—or taking Tracy to bed, not to mention Bud—affects me in a way I don't expect.

I wouldn't call it jealousy exactly. But I definitely don't like the idea.

"Let's get you a drink," Teddy says.

For an instant, I consider whether I should be drinking. Maybe I should be setting a good example for Dragon.

But you know what? He's my roommate, not my ward. He's an addict, and he has to deal with that himself. He's the one who wanted to come here. Now that Tracy knows he's an addict, she most likely won't try to sway him.

And if she does?

File that under *Not my problem.*

This is my last night to unwind for a while, and I'd like to make the most of it.

CHAPTER TWELVE

DRAGON

Sometimes I wonder if allowing myself a joint and a few beers helped me stay away from the harder stuff.

Already I'm second-guessing my decision to come along.

Because that craft beer is calling to me. And so is the marijuana, its pungent smell drifting around the room.

I used to let myself have that kind of stuff, and I kept it cool.

But this time, I promised my therapist I'd stay clean.

And that means totally clean.

No pot, no beer, no wine.

I never had a difficult time staying away from hard liquor. I don't really like the flavor, though I certainly drank my share of it when I was younger.

But beer? Wine? Pot? Allowing myself those few vices seemed to help me stay away from the hard stuff.

Not that I think anyone has narcotics at this party. This seems like a pretty tame crowd, despite the fact that Tracy is dressed like a dominatrix. Fishnet, black leather shorts, and a white blouse so sheer I can see the red tips of her nipples. One of them is pierced.

Funny. I have pierced nipples myself, but I don't really like the look on a woman.

A woman's breasts are beautiful without any adornment.

Tracy gets me a glass of water and hands it to me. "Here you go, Dragon. Do you want to dance a little?"

I take a sip of water. "Not much of a dancer."

She walks her fingers up my arm. "What do you like to do?"

"Play the drums. Read. Watch movies."

"What kind of movies do you like?"

Funny that she didn't ask what kind of books I like. Diana did at the diner. But Tracy doesn't strike me as much of a reader.

"I like the classics. They don't make movies like that anymore."

"Classics like *Pretty Woman*?"

I have to stop myself from laughing. "No. I'm talking about much older classics. One of my favorites is *Guess Who's Coming to Dinner.*"

She wrinkles her forehead. "I'm not sure I know that one. Do you like *Casablanca*?"

"Yeah, that's a good one. I also like all the old Woody Allen movies."

She wrinkles her brow again. "I'm not familiar with his work." She takes a sip of her IPA from the amber bottle.

Fuck. I can almost see the malty hops sliding over her tongue... For an instant, I want to grab her and kiss her, just for the slightest taste.

I swallow. I will always crave what I can't have. I can't change that. I wish I could, but I can't.

Funny thing is that any other night I might consider relapsing. Just a few sips of beer.

But tonight, with Diana here... I don't want to disappoint

her.

Not that I think she'd be disappointed. I don't think she cares about me one way or the other. She's letting me live at her place as a favor to Jesse and Brianna, and I appreciate it, but I certainly don't expect anything from her.

So why do I give two shits if I disappoint her?

Man, I can't stop staring at Tracy's beer.

My gaze is drawn to the amber bottle as if it's got some magnetic force. The condensation accumulating on the outside of it, and Tracy's full lips as she clasps them around it and takes a drink of the intoxicating elixir.

"Excuse me," I murmur as I head toward the door.

I don't have a clue where I'm going. I don't know this building, although Diana did say something about it having a great roof for parties.

I scan the hallway and find the stairwell. Once I'm on it, I walk up to the top and open the door.

The roof is huge—a large concrete pad. On one end is a barbecue setup, and on the other end is a bar.

No one's here, so no one is having drinks.

The sun has set, and I look up to the stars.

There are a lot of things I like about the city, but the view at night is not one of them.

Out on the western slope—without the light pollution of the city—I can see the stars so much more clearly than here. One great thing about Colorado is that we have over three hundred days of sunshine a year, and though the sky's not cloudy at all tonight, all I can see are a few speckled stars and the moon.

On the western slope, the entire sky lights up at night.

Sometimes I sit outside, especially during the summer

when it's hot, in a lounge chair and just stare at the sky for hours and hours.

It relaxes me.

Makes me realize I'm just a speck in a sea of something so much grander.

Makes my problems seem infinitesimal.

But here? First, there's no lounge chair, and second, while the moon is beautiful, it's way closer to the earth than the stars are. Some of the stars I see on the western slope are stars that burned out millennia ago and the light is just getting here.

I love the thought of it.

Just like those stars, there will come a day when I die. But maybe there's a chance that, if I continue to turn my life around, I will leave a legacy behind that outlasts my physical life. And until then, I can carry on the lights of those who have gone before me. My grandparents, for example.

Or Griffin.

I wipe a tear from my eye, chastising myself for letting my mind wander to my baby sister. Especially with an apartment full of booze and weed below me. I return my gaze to the stars.

If I ever had the chance to go to college, I would've studied astronomy. I would've also studied music. In some weird way—for me at least—the two go together.

Of course, there are songs about the stars. Lots of pop songs especially. But my mind goes to the song "The Impossible Dream" from the musical *Man of La Mancha*. The song ends with a line about reaching the unreachable star.

For a long time, my unreachable star was sobriety, a stable life.

Now I have a new one. Diana Steel.

I'm attracted to her. But I can't have her. Forget that

she's too good for me, which she definitely is. Staying in her penthouse is my one chance at getting my life together in Denver without going completely broke. I can't jeopardize that by hitting on her. She already feels unsafe with me around. Why else would she have installed that extra lock?

I breathe in, breathe out, breathe in again. Focus on the stars.

And within a few minutes, the pulsing amber bottle Tracy was holding is a distant memory.

I suppose I should go back down to the party. Diana may be wondering where I am. Or she may not.

But on the off chance she is, I don't want her to worry.

I walk to the door of the roof and—

"You've got to be kidding," I grouse out loud.

The door is—of course—locked.

How do people in this building throw parties up here if the door locks behind them?

Ah. A keycard reader. That's how they do it. My gaze falls to a couple of large bricks sitting next to the door. Right. For when no one has a keycard. I should have noticed those when I came up here.

I do have my phone, though, so I call Diana to let her know I'm up here. Good thing she insisted we exchange information.

The phone rings several times before it goes to voicemail.

Hi, this is Diana Steel. I'm sorry I can't get to the phone, but please leave your message, and I will get back to you right away.

"It's me, Dragon," I say into the phone. "I went up on the roof to get some air, and now I'm locked up here. Sorry for the inconvenience, but could you or Teddy or somebody come get me?"

She may not have heard her phone, so I text her as well, hoping she might see it.

Whatever. I guess I'm up here for a while.

I rub my arms against the chill.

I'm wearing a long-sleeved shirt, but still, it's October, and once the sun goes down, the temperature drops.

Some folding chairs are stacked in one corner alone with a few folding tables.

I grab a chair and sit, looking at the sky.

But this time it offers me no peace or solace.

Not here in the city.

I'd go back to the western slope in a minute if it weren't for my rehab.

Eventually, though, I'm going to have to trust myself not to relapse.

I don't feel ready yet, though. Not when that beer pulsated with my own heartbeat and called to me in a seductive siren's voice.

I settle in. This is nothing. I'm a little bit chilled, but it's not the worst place I've been locked in.

The judge is a large man—his skin is dark, and he wears those half glasses. He looks at me, and his eyes are saying something. He's a good man. He's trying to do what's right.

"This is the matter of Dragon Locke."

I sit with a person—a young woman with brown hair and blue eyes—who is my guardian ad litem. I don't know what that means, but I memorized the words. She sits with me while my parents sit at a different table.

The judge, whose name I can't pronounce, turns his gaze to my parents.

"Mr. and Mrs. Locke," he says gravely, "do you understand what you're about to do here?"

"We do, your honor," my father says.

"You are voluntarily giving up parental rights to your son," the judge says again.

"Yes, your honor." My father clears his throat.

"And you've discussed this with counsel, and you've come to the conclusion that it would be in the best interests of all parties involved?"

My mother sniffles, wipes her eyes with a tissue.

My mother cries a lot.

She's been crying ever since Griffin got hurt.

They've accused me of some very awful things. Things I would never do.

I don't understand a lot about what's happening. I'm barely nine years old. I'm getting to be a big boy, but all I know is that I haven't been living with my parents ever since what happened with Griffin.

I've been living in a place that locks me in.

I don't like being locked in.

It makes me angry—makes me think about doing things I know I shouldn't do. Things that I know are wrong.

The lady beside me has told me to be quiet. Not to say anything. When I look at my mother and father—the two people who used to love me the most in this world—I can't help it. I leave the table and run over to them.

"Mommy, Daddy, I'll be good. I promise I'll be good. I won't

do anything wrong ever again. Please don't make me leave. Please."

My mother doesn't look at me. She looks down at the table.

But my father does. He meets my gaze. I can't tell what he's thinking, but he does look me in the eye sternly.

Mommy always said I have Daddy's eyes, though I never understood why because his are brown and mine are different. But I used to like that he and I shared eyes. We were close. He gave me a drum.

But as I stare into those eyes now, they don't seem familiar at all.

It's almost like I'm looking at a stranger.

A stranger is a person who wants to hurt me. I learned all about strangers first from Mommy and Daddy and then from my kindergarten teacher years ago.

We don't talk to strangers.

We don't go anywhere with strangers.

Why has my daddy become a stranger?

They think I hurt Griffin.

They think I did something absolutely horrible to her.

Why don't they believe me?

Why don't they believe me when I say I would never hurt Griffin?

That I love Griffin.

That I miss her.

But she's gone now. They won't let me near her.

And I guess it's time for me to go, too.

CHAPTER THIRTEEN

DIANA

Teddy doesn't smoke pot, but most of her parties tend to have it. Tracy and Bud seem to be complete party animals, so when Teddy goes to the kitchen to refill the hors d'oeuvres, I grab her.

"You need help?" I ask.

"Yeah, if you don't mind," she says. "Do you know how to make a salami rose?"

I let out a short laugh. "You're not even going to believe this, but I do."

She scoffs. "I was asking kind of as a joke. You're not known for your cooking skills, Dee."

"I know, but my aunt is a gourmet chef, and my mother is her second-in-command, so when I'm home, I get roped into doing things just like this. And yes, I actually do know how to make a salami rose."

"I don't have to teach you, then. Great." Teddy hands me a thin highball glass.

I already know what to do. I take the round pieces of salami and bend them over the rim of the glass, slightly overlapping each piece. Once I get a couple layers going, four or five rows of salami at least, I turn the glass over and gently pull it out. The result is a gorgeous salami rose.

"Impressive," Teddy says as she slices cheese.

I make two more salami roses and then three pepperoni ones. By the time I'm done, Teddy is finished slicing cheese and pours some mixed nuts in a bowl.

She picks up the platter and eyes it. "I think you did better than I could have," she says. "Maybe there's hope for you after all, Diana."

I laugh and take another drink of my water. "I can do a good charcuterie tray. That's about it."

Teddy sets the tray back down.

"Something else you can do that makes it look really cool," I tell her, "is you can take a cookie-cutter and make a shape in the top of your brie. Pop off the white rind, and then put some jam or jelly in the shape. It's really pretty, and you can grab some of the jam when you take your brie as well."

Teddy cocks her head at me. "Who are you and what have you done with Diana Steel?"

I can't help laughing again. "I never do this kind of stuff myself. You know me. I'm kind of a loner and rarely throw parties. But my family throws the most elaborate parties on the planet."

She strokes her chin. "Maybe you missed your calling. You're really creative, Diana."

"Those are tricks stolen from my aunt Marjorie. And as far as my creativity goes, I prefer putting it into buildings and structure."

Teddy smirks. "I bet you're looking forward to starting work."

I chuckle. "I so am. If they don't let me on that mountaintop project, I don't know what I'm going to do."

"First of all, they're going to let you on." Teddy rolls her eyes. "And second of all, if they don't put you on it, then you'll work your cute little behind off until they realize they need to let you in." She sighs. "You're such a workaholic, Dee. I interviewed with L & L two years ago, and they offered me a job, but did you know they expect their assistants to work over fifty hours a week?"

I nod. "I don't doubt it. They expect even more out of their architects. But I think it'll be good for me. I'm no stranger to hard work, and if I can get on this project..."

"Just do your best, Diana."

"I always do." I open the nearest drawer. "Do you have cookie cutters?"

Teddy scratches her chin. "I have a few, but they're all Christmas themed." She opens a drawer next to the one I was looking through. In it are several cookie cutters. A tree, a gingerbread man, a candy cane... All seasonally inappropriate options.

I pick up one of the cookie cutters, this one shaped like a Santa hat. "Too bad you don't have any Halloween ones. A pumpkin would be perfect for today. But no worries. I just need a paring knife, a sharp one."

"Okay, sure." A few minutes later, Teddy hands me a paring knife.

I start to cut into the brie when— "I guess I should have asked. Do you have jam or jelly?"

Teddy frowns. "Oh... I don't." She darts her gaze around the kitchen. "But I do have some honey. It's fresh. I just bought it a few days ago."

Honey and brie. That sounds really good. "Yeah, let's try the honey."

With the paring knife, I carefully carve a pumpkin shape that turns out to look more like a big cherry, but what the hell?

Then I carefully remove the rind from the cutout and drizzle the honey into the indentation.

"This should taste really good," I say to Teddy, "and it actually looks cute, but it looks a lot better with a darker jam or jelly. You know, to contrast with the white rind."

Teddy's eyes are wide. "I don't think I've ever seen a charcuterie tray look better, Dee. Thanks for your help."

"Not a problem." I shrug. "It's kind of fun to do. Lets me flex my creative muscles in a different way."

"Well, you're a genius at it." Teddy picks up the tray. "Hey, everyone, look at this amazing piece of art that Diana and I put together."

Like vultures, the guests descend on the tray, filling up their plates.

"Hey." Teddy's friend Tracy grabs my arm.

"Yeah?"

Tracy takes another sip of her beer. "Where did your friend go off to?"

"Who? Teddy?"

"No, that guy you brought with you."

"Oh, Dragon..." I cast my gaze around the room. "I don't see him. He's probably in the bathroom."

Tracy scratches her arm. "He's not. I just checked."

I raise an eyebrow. "You checked the bathroom for a guy?"

"Well, yeah." Tracy's cheeks turn pink. "But no one was in there. I can't find him anywhere."

I look around Teddy's loft. She only has the one bedroom and bathroom. Plus this big open living area and kitchen.

"Is he seeing anyone?" Tracy continues.

"Uh..." I keep darting my gaze around. "What?"

"Your friend," Tracy says. "Is he seeing anyone?"

I swallow. "Not that I know of."

"And the two of you aren't..."

Warmth surges over my cheeks. "Oh, no. Not at all. We're just roommates. He's a friend of my brother-in-law's, and I'm letting him stay at my place. That's all."

Tracy smiles at me. "I'm glad to hear that. Because he is hot."

I can't disagree with Tracy. Dragon is hot. Classically handsome, with granite-carved facial features, amazing eyes, with the long hair and stubble that give him that dangerous look.

I've always appreciated his attractiveness, but I considered him some kind of enigma. Someone who'd be hard to get to know.

Plus I always had other things going on and wasn't interested in finding a man.

I want to work toward my career in architecture. At some point, I want to be one of those architects whose work is featured on the cover of *Architecture Digest*. The one who billion-dollar corporations hire to design their next amazing building.

Tracy is yammering at me about something, and I catch the last couple of words.

"...you think he left?"

Good question. "Let me grab my purse. I'll give him a call."

Tracy nods as I head into Teddy's bedroom where everyone's coats and purses are stashed. I grab my phone and—

"Oh, shit!"

I run out of the room and find Teddy, who's dancing with Bud. I grab her arm.

She cocks her head. "Yeah, what is it, Dee?"

"My friend I brought with me. Dragon. He went up to the roof, and now he's stuck up there."

She drops her jaw. "Oh my God. Yeah, you either have to have a keycard to open it, or most people just stick a brick in the door jamb. There's a pile of bricks." She frowns. "I wonder why he didn't do that."

"He probably didn't think of it. If I know Dragon, he probably went up to get some alone time."

She digs into her pocket. "Here, take my key. Go on up and get him."

"Thanks, Ted."

I grab my jacket from the bed and leave Teddy's apartment. I walk to the end of the hallway to the stairwell and up to the top. I open the door.

I've been to this rooftop many times, but it looks way different without people milling about, without lights strung up and glittering.

The air is brisk now that the sun has gone down. The moon is high in the sky. I look around. "Dragon?"

There are a few alcoves on the roof, so I check them.

But when I don't find Dragon—

I gasp out in panic.

"Dragon!" I say loudly.

No response.

Okay... No need to panic. Maybe he found another way down. Maybe someone came up and opened the door and he got out that way.

But if he'd done that, wouldn't he have come back to the party? Or at least told me where he was going?

Maybe not.

This is Dragon, after all. He would probably feel like he

was bothering me. He has his own key to my place, so he may have just gone home.

I grab my phone and call my landline. He may not answer, but at least it's a shot.

But now it rings five times and then goes to my voice messaging system.

Dragon's the dark brooding type—that much is for sure. But there's no way in hell he would... My stomach twists.

I walk to the edge of the roof. Nausea curls through my throat as I look down.

Nobody splattered on the road, thank God.

I check the other side. There are only two edges since the building is attached to other structures on either side.

How could he have gotten down?

There are fire escapes outside all the loft windows.

I check again.

Sure enough, on the back of the building, there's a small fire escape.

I breathe a sigh of relief. That must be how he got down, but... Wouldn't he let me know he got off the roof?

Something's not right here.

I let myself back into the building using Teddy's card and walk back down the stairs to the floor to her loft.

The party is still going strong, and the smell of marijuana is seeping out through her door.

Nothing to do about that. It's legal here in Colorado. The smell of weed is everywhere, especially on the weekends.

I hate the sickeningly sweet smell, but I've gotten more used to it since I've been living here in town.

I find Teddy quickly and give her back her card. "I need to go. He's not up on the roof, and he hasn't texted me or called me."

Teddy furrows her brow. "He's a grown man, Dee."

"True that." I run my hands through my hair. "But I also called my place. He didn't answer the landline."

Teddy shrugs. "Because it's *your* landline. He probably thinks he shouldn't be doing that. For all he knows, you might get personal and private calls on it."

I shake my head. "I hardly use the landline. I only have it because it is cheaper to bundle my TV, phone line, and internet service than it is to pay for them à la carte."

"Yeah, I do it too. A silly reason, but I have one." She grabs my hands. "I want you to stay, Dee. The party's just getting started."

"I'd like to." I gaze toward Teddy's front door. "I don't drink much, but I was considering tying one on tonight since it's my last chance for a while."

Teddy pouts her lips. "Don't think of it that way. Reserve Saturday nights for yourself, Diana."

Teddy means well, but she's not an architect. She's an executive assistant, and she's gone as far in the firm as she's going to go.

She has a point, though. I do need to take care of myself, because if I don't, I won't have the best to give to my new firm.

"Tell you what," I say. "Once I figure out where Dragon is, I'll come back. It's still early."

"Yeah. We'll be going well past midnight." She squeezes my hands. "I hope I see you again tonight."

"You will."

Then I leave.

And I wonder where the fuck Dragon could have gone.

CHAPTER FOURTEEN

DRAGON

I'm back at the diner, and it's not nearly as crowded at this hour, though it is open twenty-four hours, so people are still here eating.

Lexi's off duty, but another server I know, Carmen, is taking care of me.

"Coffee?" she asks.

"No. I have enough trouble sleeping as it is." I yawn. "Another slice of that awesome cherry pie and some ice water, please."

The other great thing about this diner is they don't serve liquor. They're a true old-fashioned diner, where you can get basic food and ice cream desserts. In fact...

"Give me a chocolate malt too, Carmen."

"You got it." She winks at me. "I'll be back."

Chocolate malt and cherry pie. I really was lying when I told Diana I don't go for sweets. Luckily I don't gain weight easily. I probably didn't need both. Since I already had cherry pie once today, I probably should have just gone for the chocolate malt.

But there are times...

Times when I need something to do with my mouth. Because what my mouth really wants to do is smoke a joint.

Suck on a beer bottle.

Or take a few pills.

Anything to get my head out of where it is.

I grab my phone.

A call from Diana.

I should call her, tell her I'm fine. Tell her I got off the roof.

I found the fire escape and climbed down. Nearly broke my neck in the process, but I made it. I thought about heading back to her place, or even back to the party... But my own thoughts plagued me, ate at me, so I'm back at the diner, where I can get something to put in my mouth that won't make me high.

Except maybe a sugar high.

I have an emergency number for my therapist. He'll take my call day or night if I need him to. He lets me do that because he knows I won't abuse the privilege. I've only called twice since I got out of rehab.

Once, the day before the wedding, when I had to go to the rehearsal dinner, and then the wedding itself, where the booze would be flowing.

Then once again, after the wedding, to tell him I did fine and also ask his advice on whether I should move back to Denver.

We talked it through, and it turned out what I really needed to do was move back to Denver. Be away from my home on the western slope.

Be away from a lot of things.

A lot of memories.

I didn't grow up on the western slope. I ended up there after I reached adulthood and got kicked out of the system.

I actually grew up in the suburbs of Denver.

That's where my parents washed their hands of me, made me a ward of the state.

I always wondered why Griffin never told them the truth once she came out of shock.

Told them I wasn't the one who hurt her.

Didn't matter anyway.

Once they sent me away, they lost Griffin as well.

"Here you go." Carmen slides a chocolate malt, a piece of cherry pie, and a glass of ice water in front of me. "You may need a downer after that sugar rush you're going to get."

I chuckle humorlessly. "My whole life is a downer, Carmen."

She twists her lips into a frown. "I don't like to hear you talk like that, Dragon. Everything's fine. Count your blessings, my friend."

Blessings?

I do have a few.

"That's good advice, Carmen."

I should say thank you, but I have such a hard time with those two words. Which is strange because I am truly grateful for a lot of things. Grateful to Jesse and the band for not turning their backs on me when I fucked up the tour. Grateful to Diana for letting me stay at her place. Grateful to Emerald Phoenix for seeing our band in that bar, seeing something in us that we weren't sure anyone would ever see.

And I'm grateful that I have a few bucks in my pocket—enough to pay for some pie, a malt, and a nice tip for Carmen.

I take a bite of pie, letting the buttery crust float on my tongue for a moment. The tartness of the cherries complements the crust so well, and a scoop of vanilla ice cream would be the cherry on top, no pun intended.

I should've ordered a vanilla malt. The chocolate flavor is probably going to clash with the pie.

I finish the pie first. Then I go to work on the malt.

The hour gets later and later... If I'm going to call Tim, I should probably do it now.

I punch his number in.

"Dragon?" Tim says into the phone, his voice sounding like I woke him up. "Are you doing all right?"

"Did I wake you?"

"I just nodded off. But we're good. What can I help you with?"

I close my eyes and rub my forehead. "I came close tonight. I went to a party where of course there was drinking, and a lot of pot. Things I used to allow myself. I really wanted a beer, Tim."

"Sounds like you resisted, though."

"I did." I sigh. "But it wasn't easy."

"Nothing worth having is ever easy," Tim says. "You know that as well as I do."

"It's just..." I take a deep breath in before continuing. "Ever since I got sober, and I mean really sober this time, I've had these thoughts. Thoughts I've been able to keep at bay for so long."

"About your sister."

It's a statement, not a question. Tim knows. Tim knows me as well as anyone now. I still have a few secrets, but Tim knows as much as Jesse Pike knows plus a little more.

"Yeah. I'm staying with the sister of my best friend's wife. She's an heiress. A beef-ranching heiress, and she's letting me stay at her place out of the goodness of her heart. She's not charging me or anything. She has a penthouse in this great building, and I have my own private room and bathroom, plus access to all the amenities, like this awesome workout room."

"That sounds like a good thing."

"Yeah, it is. I wasn't even going to do it, and it seemed like she was just as glad, but then she kind of asked me to. Said I could stay with her."

"That's great."

"Is it though?" I scratch the side of my face. "I can't pay her. Not till the band gets moving again."

"Right. I get it."

"I don't have any talent to do anything other than drumming, so I want to get some private students, but I don't even know how to do that."

"There are websites you can hang out a shingle on," Tim says.

"I know, but still, that'll take time. I don't really have time." I absentmindedly scoot the leftover crumbs on my plate around with my fork. "I think I should maybe just get a job."

"You could do that, but you'll have to quit as soon as your band gets back together."

"Yeah. I know. If I were home on the western slope, I could do odd jobs. That's pretty much how I made a living—well, that and the dispensary—and I had the flexibility to play with the band as well."

"You could do odd jobs here."

"How? Again, I'd have to go on some website and advertise my services. Back home, everybody knew me and always knew to call me when they needed something done."

"Dragon, what's this really about?" Tim says, his tone a bit pissy.

I breathe in a deep breath and decide to admit something

that I've barely admitted to myself. "This woman I'm staying with. Diana Steel. I find myself... I'm attracted to her. I mean, really attracted to her. In a way that I'm not sure I've ever been attracted to anyone. I've never even had a real relationship. Always figured I was too fucked up for that."

"Finding a woman attractive doesn't have to be a bad thing, Dragon."

I sigh. "She's way out of my league. She's gorgeous and rich and smart and amazing. And I'm just..."

"You're a good man, Dragon. You know that. Your past doesn't have to rule your life. You've done a good job with that so far."

I roll my eyes. "Yeah... When I was allowed to have a beer or a toke every now and then."

"You're an enigma for sure," Tim says. "Most addicts can't control themselves the way you did. But I honestly think that if you had gone stone-cold sober, cold turkey, the first time, you probably wouldn't have had that relapse in London."

I nod, knowing Tim can't see me. We've had this discussion before. I don't know that I agree with him, but he's the expert.

"I shouldn't have gone to the party," I say.

"Why do you say that?"

I frown. "I'm clearly not ready to be around drugs."

"You made it to the rehearsal dinner and wedding."

"I did, but that was just alcohol. It's easier to decline alcohol. Drugs are another story. Something about being high... It just takes all the shit in the world away."

"But it doesn't," he says.

"Yeah, I know. It's temporary."

"Tell me more about the woman you're living with. About these feelings you're having."

"Feelings?" I scoff into the phone. "They're not *feelings*, Tim. I'm attracted to her. I get a hard-on when she's around. If you saw her, you would too."

Tim chuckles. "Are you forgetting that I'm gay?"

"No. I'm saying she's *that* goddamned beautiful."

He pauses a moment. "You sure it's just attraction? That there are no feelings involved?"

"Of course I'm sure," I huff. "I hardly know the woman."

"You must know her well enough to feel comfortable living in her home."

"It's either that or be homeless."

"Except that's not true, Dragon. There are other options. You and I both know that."

Tim's usually right.

"Yeah..." I take a sip of my water before I continue. "I'm sorry to bother you. This isn't really something I need your input on. I mean, I thought it was, but..."

"Dragon, you're not one to misuse your privilege of having my private phone. So the fact that you called me is something in itself. There *is* something bothering you. And it has something to do with your new roommate because she is the new factor in this equation."

"I'm attracted to a woman. Big deal, right?"

"You want to try for a relationship with this woman?" Tim asks.

"God, no. She'd never have me."

"What makes you think that?"

"If you could see her, you'd know."

"You're an attractive man, Dragon. Hell, you'll probably be a bona fide rock star soon."

"If they let me back in the band."

"They've already let you back in the band," he reminds me.

He doesn't need to remind me. I know that. And I'm eternally grateful for it. Apparently, the substitute drummer they hired made it clear he'd be happy to take my place in the band. Jesse and the others said hell no.

"I don't know what it is," I say. "Maybe I just have more demons to slay."

"Some demons you never slay," Tim says, his tone serious. "Some you just have to learn to live with."

CHAPTER FIFTEEN

DIANA

When I get back to my place, my phone finally dings.

I heave a sigh of relief when I see Dragon's name.

At the diner.

At the diner?

That's it?

Nothing about how he got off the roof? Nothing about being sorry he worried me?

Christ.

"You're totally serious," I say out loud.

I press on his name, dialing him.

"Yeah?" he says into my ear.

"It's me, Dragon. Diana."

"I know. I see your name on the caller ID."

"For crying out loud," I say. "Everyone was worried."

"If you were that worried, you would've answered your phone when I told you I was stuck on the roof."

"My phone was in my purse, which was in Teddy's bedroom. It's not like I carry it around at parties. I was trying to be social, not buried in my phone."

"Most of the people there had their phones out."

I ball my hands into fists. "For God's sake, this isn't about me, Dragon. It's about you. You could've let me know you weren't coming back to the party once you got off the roof. Teddy and I were looking for you."

"You didn't look that far. The diner's about a block away from Teddy's place."

"That's not even the point."

"That's exactly the point, Diana. You're not my keeper."

"You texted me saying you were stuck on the roof," I say through gritted teeth. "That makes me your keeper. You were asking for help. I came to give you help."

"Not quick enough, so I found another way."

"Didn't you think you should have let me know? Didn't you realize I would eventually get your text and wonder if you were freezing your ass off up on the roof?"

He says nothing then.

Good. Maybe I knocked some sense into that hard head of his.

Until—

"I don't have to tell you where I'm going."

"Oh, for God's sake, here we go again. It's just common courtesy, Dragon. I came to let you off the roof, and you weren't there. You didn't end up back at the party, so it was common courtesy to let me know where you were so I wouldn't worry."

"You weren't really worrying anyway."

His words should be the truth. He's a grown man, and I'm not his keeper. He's right about that. So yeah, I shouldn't have been worrying.

But I was.

I mean... If something happened to him, Jesse and Brianna would never forgive me.

"Look," I say. "We're going to have to come to some agreement. If we're somewhere together, and you decide to leave, let me know. It's common courtesy. That's all I ask."

He sighs. "I didn't exactly decide to leave, Diana. I got locked up on the roof, and no one came to help me. So I helped myself. That's a good thing."

Yes, it's a good thing. I'm tempted to yell at him some more, but he probably learned all that shit in rehab. That you have to help yourself.

I don't want to fuck up his rehab or his therapy.

Maybe it was too hard for him to be around the booze and the pot tonight.

Maybe I need to be more understanding.

"Fine," I say. "I'm heading back to Teddy's. That's where I'll be if you need me."

"Okay. I guess I'll see you when you get home, then."

"I guess so. Bye, Dragon." This time I slide my phone into the pocket of my jeans. It's on vibrate, so I should be able to feel it if he calls.

This shouldn't drive me as crazy as it does. I shouldn't feel responsible for him.

If I'm being honest with myself, I'm feeling something more than just responsibility because of Brianna and Jesse.

And I don't like it.

I don't like it one bit.

So I'm going back to the party.

I'm going to have a drink. Maybe even two drinks.

And if I find a nice warm body to cuddle up with for the night? All the better.

I haven't had sex in nearly a year, and I think it's time.

I have to pound hard on the door for Teddy to let me in. The party is raging strong—the number of people here has tripled—and the smell of pot is more pungent than ever.

I'm not a beer drinker, so I head to the kitchen and pour myself a glass of whatever red they're pouring.

Then I shake my head.

It's the Colorado Pike red blend, made by my brother-in-law's family.

They won't have any wine releases for the next few years since a fire destroyed their winery and vineyards a year ago.

The Pikes make table wines. Easily drinkable wines that don't cost an arm and a leg, unlike my uncle Ryan and my brother Dale. They make top-of-the-line wines.

I take a sip.

It's good.

I don't know much about wine—my brother has tried to educate me, but I'm a lost cause because I'm just not really into alcohol—but this is quite delicious. It's easy to drink. It tastes of red fruit with just a touch of vanilla.

But other than that? It just tastes nice. It's easy on my tongue, goes down my throat smoothly.

It would be good with food. With pizza, actually.

We don't have any pizza here, but I can remedy that in a moment. Normally I wouldn't be so presumptuous, but I know Teddy won't mind.

I pull up my food delivery app—unconsciously checking to see if Dragon has texted; he hasn't—take a look around the room to assess the number of pizzas I need, and then order six large pizzas—three pepperoni, three cheese—to be delivered to Teddy's place.

It's Saturday night, so I pay the extra fee for rush delivery.

Excellent. Twenty minutes and they'll be here. I sip the wine slowly so I'll still have a nearly full glass when the pizza gets here.

In the meantime, I take a look around. The two friends of Teddy's who are in town—Tracy and Bud—are deep in conversation with two young women.

Teddy is talking to a handsome young man, and there are a couple of other groups of women and men chatting about, and then I see him...

A man by himself in the corner checking his phone.

He's tall with light-brown hair, and he's wearing faded jeans and a plaid flannel shirt. So not my type.

Which is why I take another sip of my wine and walk toward him.

He looks up at me as I draw near.

"Am I interrupting you?" I ask.

"No. I was just returning a text." He holds out his hand. "I'm Antonio, by the way."

I shake his hand. "Diana." I look him up and down. "You don't look like an Antonio."

He cocks his head. "I don't?"

"Antonios are supposed to be the dark Latin type. Dark hair, dark eyes, tanned skin."

"I'm Italian," he says. "Northern Italian."

"What's your last name?"

"Carbone. What's yours?"

"Steel."

As usual, I get the wide eyes at that. "Not the Steels?"

I bite my lip. "Guilty."

My family is well known in Colorado. They're pretty much known nationwide. But Steel isn't an uncommon name, so it always boggles my mind that people just assume I'm one of the Steels.

"So I assume you work for your family?" Antonio asks.

I shake my head. "I'm an architect."

He lifts an eyebrow. "You mean your rich family doesn't dabble in architecture? They have their hands in just about everything else."

I decide not to take his comment the wrong way because I don't think he means it to be rude. He's right. The elders of my family are way more than just ranchers. You don't become billionaires simply by ranching.

"They do *not* have their fingers in the architecture game," I say. "I've gotten there on my own."

"That's cool." He smiles. "Good for you."

There's something patronizing about what he just said, but again, I don't think he meant it that way. Sometimes people just don't know how to act when I tell them who my family is.

"What do you do?" I ask him.

"I own a music store," he says. "It's right on the outskirts of downtown. I sing and play guitar nights and weekends, but I'm off tonight."

My interest is piqued. "A music store? Do you offer instruction?"

"Yeah, of course. You looking to learn to sing or play an instrument?"

"God, no," I laugh. "I have no musical talent at all. But my roommate is a drummer. I know he'd like to get some students."

"Really?" He strokes his chin. "Percussion is very popular. We can always use new instructors. What are his qualifications?"

"He's a member of the band Dragonlock. They just went on tour with Emerald Phoenix."

This time his jaw drops. "No shit? Yeah, have him call me." He pulls a card out of his pocket and hands it to me. "I wouldn't mind if *you* called me either, Diana." He gives me a smile.

"Maybe I will." I smile back at him. He's quite handsome, with broad shoulders, narrow hips. I'm so used to guys from the western slope. This guy has yuppie written all over him, despite his flannel shirt.

I'm about to open my mouth to ask more about his music store when Teddy comes strolling up.

"Hey, Dee, I see you met my cousin."

This time *I* widen my eyes. "You guys are cousins?"

"Yeah," Antonio says. "Guilty. Our mothers are sisters."

"How have I not met you before now?" I ask. "I interned at Teddy's architecture firm."

"I'm not one for parties," Antonio says. "But my good cousin here convinced me to come to this one since Tracy and Bud were coming into town."

"So you know Tracy and Bud too?"

"Oh, yeah. We all went to college together."

"So much I don't know." I twirl a lock of my hair and give Antonio a slight smile.

Teddy looks at me and then at Antonio, and then back at me. "Something going on with you two?"

"Of course not," I say, my cheeks warming.

But then Antonio looks at me, and I see the color of his eyes. They're not brown as I originally thought, but greenish brown.

Hazel, like Dragon's.

Except not anything like Dragon's. I don't see flecks of gold or...

Why am I thinking of Dragon Locke's eyes?

"That's too bad," Antonio says. "I thought we were getting along pretty well."

"Never say never, Dee." Teddy turns at some pounding on the door. "I wonder who that can be."

"Those are the pizzas I ordered," I say.

Teddy raises an eyebrow. "Pizza?"

"Yeah." I swirl the remaining wine in my glass. "I had a craving for pizza to go with this wine. I figured you'd be okay with it. I ordered enough for everybody."

"Of course it's okay, but you didn't have to do that, Diana. I have more stuff in the fridge for another charcuterie platter."

"Oh, Teds," Antonio says, laughing. "We all love your charcuterie, but come on. There's no substitute for pizza."

Teddy chuckles lightheartedly as she goes to the door, grabs the pizzas, takes them into the kitchen, and sets them out on her small counter.

"Hey, everyone," she yells over the music. "We got some pizza!"

The pot smokers descend like vultures, which I expected.

I manage to grab a piece of pepperoni for myself before it's gone. Then I find an empty chair in the corner, sit down with what remains of my glass of wine, and take a bite of the pizza.

The creamy cheese and the spice of the pepperoni...so good. Then I take a sip of the wine.

Mmm, delicious with the tomato sauce. It must be made of an acidic grape. That's what Dale says. A wine that has a high acidity goes well with food, especially tomatoes.

Whatever. All I know is it tastes damned good, and once I'm finished with my pizza and I've drunk the last of my wine, I go to pour another glass.

And who should be getting a glass himself? Antonio Carbone.

"The pizzas didn't last long," he says.

"I know." I wave the stench of marijuana away from in front of me. "All the pot smoking. They all have the munchies. But I only wanted one piece of pepperoni, and I got it."

He scratches the side of his head. "You paid for all those pizzas and only got one piece?"

I shrug.

He presses his lips together. "Oh right... You're an heiress."

I roll my eyes. "I'm not just an heiress. I'm a human being. My own person. I'm an architect."

"Yes, you are. An architect who bought six pizzas so she could have one slice." He chuckles as he takes the bottle of wine and pours some into my glass. "Teddy tells me you're starting a new job."

"First thing Monday morning."

"Congratulations." He clinks his glass to mine.

"Thank you." I take a sip of the wine. There are a few straggler pieces of pizza left, all cheese. I pick up a napkin and grab one, despite the fact that I may pay for it tomorrow. "Now I'm an architect who bought six pizzas so she could have two slices. Much more economical." I smile. "You'd better have another while you can."

"Oh, I don't eat pizza. I'm a vegan."

I drop my jaw.

"Never met a vegan before?"

"No, of course I have. You just don't run into too many

vegans where I come from."

He nods slowly. "Not in a family whose company is based on beef, I suppose."

Christ, can we stop talking about my family? I'm trying to flirt here.

"Tell me about your veganism," I say. "What made you make that decision?"

He smiles. "I just love animals."

"I love animals too."

"Yeah, I know. You don't have to be a vegan to love animals." His smile vanishes. "I just really hate the food industry. The inhumane way they're treated."

"Our animals have a really good life," I say. "My dad and uncles pride themselves on that. They're grass fed, and they graze freely."

"But they still end up on someone's plate."

I frown. "They do."

I take another sip of my wine. I need to find someone else if I think I'm going to get laid tonight. I like Antonio well enough, but since he seems to have a problem with everything my family does for a living, he's probably not the wisest choice.

I take one more sip of wine. "It was great meeting you, Antonio. Excuse me."

He grabs my arm gently. "Does it bother you that I'm a vegan?"

I shake my head. "Of course not. Does it bother you that my family makes a living raising beef?"

"No." He looks at the floor. "I'm sorry if I came off as judgmental. This is just my personal choice. I don't look down on anyone who eats meat."

I smile then. Maybe he is a nice guy after all. "I certainly respect your decisions, and I'm glad you respect mine."

"I do. So..." He glances around the room. The party has begun to die down. "You want to get out of here?"

I'm feeling something. Definitely a little bit of horniness. Probably because I've had two glasses of wine, which is a lot for me.

And he *is* attractive.

"Sure," I say. "What did you have in mind?"

"My place is up north, in Westminster," he says. "Where's your place?"

I swallow. "A few blocks away. But I have to warn you. I don't keep any alcohol in the house."

"Did I ask for alcohol?" He smiles.

"No."

"We can just talk."

I roll my eyes at him. "I've heard that before."

He puts a hand up in front of him. "You're a friend of Teddy's. And I don't use women. So we go to your place. We talk alone. If something happens, great. If nothing happens, great. Maybe we'll see each other again. Maybe we won't. There's no pressure, Diana." He shrugs. "It's just two people who met and want to get to know each other a little better."

When he puts it that way...

"Okay, why not? Let me just tell Teddy I'm out of here."

"We'll go together," he says.

And I smile.

I feel okay about this.

CHAPTER SIXTEEN

DRAGON

Some demons you never slay. Some you just have to learn to live with.

Tim's words haunt me as I walk around downtown Denver.

It's nearing midnight, and the clubs are hopping, and of course the smell of marijuana is on every corner.

You can't escape it in Colorado, especially on a Saturday night.

That second piece of cherry pie and my chocolate malt are heavy in my stomach. Not a good idea. I've never been one to substitute food for alcohol or drugs, so I'm not sure what got into me tonight.

Going to the party with Diana... Having that woman, Tracy, flirt all over me as she sucked on an IPA bottle.

Was it her lips on the amber rim? Or was it the beer itself?

Because Tracy was hot for sure, and she dressed like she'd be up for anything.

Still...aside from the malty beverage, all I've been thinking about is...Diana.

How attracted I am to her.

I'm going to have to find another place to stay.

But first I have to find a job—at least for a few months, until the band is back in business. We're not booked for anything else yet, and we couldn't take anything anyway until Jesse and Rory get back from their honeymoons. Brock and Rory went back to Europe and are going to be gone for at least two months. Jesse and Brianna are hanging on a beach in Jamaica, and they won't be back anytime soon either.

Part of me wants to go home. Hang out with Cage and Jake, the other two members of the band. Except the two of them like to drink as much as anyone.

I'm better off here with Diana. Diana, who doesn't keep booze in the house and rarely drinks herself.

As I walk by a twenty-four-hour liquor store, its neon sign pulses at me in sync with my heartbeat.

It says *liquor.*

But to me it pulses with different words.

Dragon...

Come in...

I'm waiting for you...

All you have to do is grab the door handle...

Open the door...

I'm waiting...waiting...waiting...

Come in, Dragon...

You know you want to...

Want to...

Want to...

I force myself to pass, to ignore the yearning to walk in, grab a six-pack of some mellow IPA, and drown myself in it.

How long have I been walking? I don't have a clue. I pull out my phone. It's after midnight now, and I've walked all through downtown Denver. I'm getting into the seedy area toward the north.

A young lady stops me in my path. "Looking for a date?"

She's a pretty young thing. I'm not even sure she's of age.

Blond hair, smoking-hot body, but there's something worn about her. Her face is so made up that she looks like a fucking clown.

"No," I say.

She walks alongside me. "You sure? I can make you forget your troubles."

If only.

I'd grab her, take her roughly behind the building, and pay her whatever she asked if I thought that were actually true.

"No," I say again.

Then she steps in front of me, her eyes wide and pleading. "I've got to bring in some cash tonight. If I don't..."

If she doesn't, what? Her pimp will beat the shit out of her?

"No."

She grabs my arm. "Please. I have to."

God, she looks so much like...

No. I don't know what Griffin would look like as an adult. This woman has blond hair and blue eyes, but I know nothing after that. Still, the look in the young woman's eyes pulls at me. It's one of desperation—a look I know well.

I pull out my wallet. I still have some cash. I don't want this woman to get beat up because I'm turning her down. "Look," I tell her. "This is for you. I'm not going to do anything with you, but take this. Maybe it will save you for tonight. But after that, get the hell out of here. Go back to school. You're better than this."

She takes the money from me, and then her eyes widen. She turns tail and scampers off into a nearby alley.

I turn around. Headlights are on me. A car.

A police car.

And a cop.

Two cops.

Within seconds, my face is pushed into a brick wall. "You're under arrest for solicitation," one cop says.

"What? You've got to be kidding me. I was trying to *help* the woman."

"We saw money exchange hands."

"Just ask her. I told her it wasn't for—"

"Did you get her?" the cop holding me asks the other one.

"She darted into a shadow. Sorry. I lost her."

"Fuck it all," I grit out.

So the little hooker's gone, and she can't validate my story.

"You have the right to remain silent," the first cop says. "Anything you say can and will be held against you in a court of law. You have the right to an attorney. If you can't afford an attorney, one will be provided for you. Do you understand these rights?"

"I didn't fucking do anything. I was trying to help her."

He nudges me into the wall. "Answer me. You understand your rights?"

"Yes," I say through clenched teeth. "Now what?"

"Now, we take you to the station. We fingerprint you. And we stick you in a holding cell until someone comes to bail you out. If no one comes, you'll be arraigned on Monday."

Monday? I'm not sitting in a jail cell until Monday. "I want my phone call."

"I'm not sure you're in any position to be making demands."

Fuck. Just what I need. In the shitstorm that has been my life, one thing I've avoided is the inside of a jail cell.

Until now, apparently.

CHAPTER SEVENTEEN

DIANA

Antonio is the perfect gentleman walking to my place. He doesn't so much as try to hold my hand.

Which is actually fine with me.

Once I let us in, I look around. "Looks like my roommate's not home yet."

"The drummer?"

"Yeah, but let me just check." I walk through the foyer and down the hallway to Dragon's room. His door is closed. I knock softly. "Dragon?"

No reply. I knock a little louder.

Then I crack the door.

It's not locked, which means he's probably not home yet.

Just to be sure, I look inside and flip the light switch.

Nope, no Dragon.

I return to Antonio. "He's not home yet."

He raises his eyebrows in a teasing gesture. "Guess we'll have the place to ourselves, then."

I tug on my lip. I don't want to be worried about Dragon, but it's after midnight at this point.

"I'll just give him a call."

I call him. No answer. I'm tempted to text him, but then I don't.

He's a grown man. I am not his keeper. That's what he told me, and he's right.

"Like I said," I say to Antonio. "I don't keep any alcohol in the house. But I do have some sparkling water and several kinds of juice."

"Sparkling water's fine."

I open the fridge. "I also have some fruit if you're hungry."

"I'm good. Teddy always keeps lots of fruit on hand when I visit."

I pour two glasses of sparkling water, squeeze a lemon into each, and hand one to Antonio as I lead him into the living room.

We sit together on my leather couch.

Now what? I take a sip of my water. I had two glasses of wine, so I'm feeling a tiny bit buzzed but not enough to just launch myself into his arms.

Even though I'm still feeling kind of horny.

"Would you like to watch a movie?" I ask.

He narrows his eyes. "I think what I'd like to do is this." He puts his glass of water down on my coffee table, setting it on a coaster. And he takes mine from me, setting it on another coaster.

A guy who uses coasters. I'm impressed.

Then he grabs my hand, cups my cheek with his other. "This is what I'd like to do, Diana." He comes close to me, and I close my eyes, ready to feel my lips against his, when—

My phone buzzes in my pocket.

I pull back. "Sorry." I grab my phone.

"Ignore it," he says.

"I'm not the kind of person who can just ignore her phone." I look at it.

It's not a number I recognize.

What the hell? I'll take his advice. Ignore it.

I set the phone on the coffee table and smile at Antonio. "Now, where were we?"

"Right about here, I think." He cups both my cheeks this time and he moves closer.

I close my eyes, and just as his lips touch mine—

My phone again.

Blaring at me from the coffee table.

"Ignore it," he says again.

"I can't."

Again, the same number that I don't recognize.

But why would whoever it is keep calling me back? And at this hour, as well?

My curiosity gets the better of me.

I place a finger on Antonio's lips. "Let me just tell them to knock it off. Then I swear I'm yours for the evening." I accept the call and bring the phone to my ear. "Hello?"

"Hi, Diana."

Dragon's voice.

"What is it? I don't recognize this number."

"That's because...I'm in jail."

I stand up, drop my jaw and my phone at the same time, and the phone clatters onto the coffee table.

Antonio rises as well. "Are you okay?"

I stand, paralyzed and numb.

This isn't happening. I've had two glasses of wine. I can't...

"Diana..." Antonio again.

He picks up my phone and hands it to me.

I put it back to my ear.

"Diana? Are you there? Damn it!"

"I'm here," I say, my lips trembling. "What kind of trouble have you gotten yourself into, Dragon?"

"I didn't do anything. You have to believe me."

"What have you been arrested for?"

"Soliciting."

"Soliciting what?" I ask, but I know the answer already. Soliciting a prostitute. What the hell was he thinking?

"I didn't do it. A woman asked if I wanted to have some fun, I told her no, she badgered me, told me she had to go back with something, so I decided to be a good Samaritan and hand her some money. And of course, two cops saw the transaction and thought I was giving her money for sex."

"Can't the hooker corroborate your story?"

"She ran off," he says. "I didn't know who else to call. Jesse's on his honeymoon, and my therapist... Well, let's just say I've bothered him enough tonight."

"Isn't he paid to be bothered by you?"

"You know what? Forget I called."

"Wait wait wait! God, Dragon, don't hang up. Where are you?"

"The police station," he says. "In a holding cell."

"Fine. I'll come get you."

"When?" he asks.

Seriously? I'm offering to come get him in the middle of the night when he's been arrested, and he asks when?

"Soon as I can get there. Christ."

"Okay. See you later."

I end the call and turn to Antonio. "I guess I'm going to go bail my roommate out of jail."

Antonio widens his eyes. "I'll take you."

"You don't have to. I'll call an Uber, go over there, and

Uber back home."

"Don't you have a car?"

"I do, but I don't mess with parking in the city. Especially at this hour. Street parking will be impossible by the police station. Rideshare is usually easier."

"I'll come with you."

"This is hardly your problem."

"I'm not sure it's yours either, Diana."

He's right about that, but the thought of Dragon sitting in a smelly holding cell with a bunch of vagrants makes me sick to my stomach.

Do I believe his story?

I do, actually. I don't think he would solicit a prostitute. At least not on purpose.

I grab my phone and pull up the ridesharing app. Saturday night downtown, there are lots of rides available, so I get one quickly.

"He's a minute away," I say.

"Okay. Let's go."

I open my mouth to say no, but then I think better. Why not have someone come with me? It's late at night.

I'll get Dragon out.

And then he's going to have to find another place to live.

CHAPTER EIGHTEEN

DRAGON

Funny thing about me.

Even after all the fuckups I've made in my life, I've never been arrested before.

I've come close, for sure. God knows, when I was still drinking and on drugs, I drove way more often than I should have.

But I never got caught, never hurt anyone in the process.

Because I don't hurt people. Well, not anymore.

I never hurt Griffin.

I heard her screams. I went to her room. I saw the bloody knife. I picked it up. Everything became a blur after that.

I'm not actually in jail. I'm in a holding cell at the police station.

After I got here, they took all my information from my driver's license and fingerprinted me.

Apparently, for certain misdemeanors, including soliciting prostitution, the City and County of Denver has preset bail amounts based on the severity of the offense. They gave me a paper, showing me the schedule.

Needless to say, I couldn't afford it, which is why I had to call Diana.

Not only is she giving me a place to stay for free, but now

I'm going to owe her for this bail money.

Of course, I'll get the bail money back, once I either cop a plea, have a trial, or, in the best circumstance, get the charges dropped altogether.

But they won't release me from custody until someone pays the bail.

At least the person I'm staying with is an heiress with unlimited cash funds.

Man, I wouldn't have blamed her if she'd told me to get fucked.

I gave that hooker all my cash. All because she reminded me of Griffin.

What Griffin might look like today.

Fuck me.

I've thought about Griffin a lot. Especially during rehab. I didn't have a choice. I had to face some shit about my life that I had stuck on the back burner for far too long.

Now that I've faced it? I wish I could shove it back into the corners of my brain.

This tiny holding cell smells like cat piss. There are only three of us in here, and I'm pretty sure the stench is coming from the guy with no teeth. The other guy is thin and agitated. He's pacing the cell like he's waiting for a bomb to drop.

I'm sitting on the bench, rubbing the ache in my forehead.

I guess I need an attorney. I can't afford an attorney, but what the hell? Diana's brother is a lawyer, but he's on his honeymoon. Not that he'd represent me anyway.

I jerk upward when an officer unlocks the cell. "Locke?"

I rise. "Yeah."

"Let's go."

Thank God. Diana must have paid my bail.

The officer leads me to a small room where he gives me back my wallet, my phone, and my jacket. Then he makes me sign a paper guaranteeing I will come back for my court appearance in two weeks.

"You understand if you don't appear, your bail will be forfeited, and we'll issue a warrant for your arrest."

I sign my name. "Yeah, yeah, yeah. I know how these things work."

"Good."

He rises. I follow him out into the lobby, where I see Diana standing with a man I don't recognize.

"Hey," I say.

"You ready?" Her voice is far from friendly.

I look the man up and down. "Who's this?"

"Antonio. He's a friend of mine."

Antonio puts out his hand.

I shake it. "Charmed," I say dryly.

"Let's go," Diana says. "The car is waiting."

"Okay."

I should thank her. And I will thank her.

Who's this idiot she's with?

I don't like seeing her with a man.

She's way too good for me, but still...

We end up home at her place, and she tells me to go on up.

I turn around and stare at Antonio. Glare at him is more like it.

It doesn't seem to faze him. Finally, I head up, using my own keycard to get into the building.

Then into the elevator and up to her place.

I open the door with my key, flip on the lights, head to the kitchen to pour myself a glass of water, and then go straight to my bedroom.

What a fucking night.

I turn the shower on, ready to wash all the grime of this day away from me, when I hear a knock on the door.

I head back, open it.

Diana stands there.

"Hey," I say.

She bites her lip. "Look, Dragon—"

"Where's your friend?" My voice is pointed. I don't mean for it to be—after all, this is the woman who literally bailed me out of jail—but I don't like the idea of Diana enjoying the company of another man.

"I sent him home." She scratches her arm. "But we need to—"

I put a hand up. "Hey, I'm innocent. I didn't give that girl money for sex. I'm not pulling your leg, Diana. Do you really think I would do something so stupid?"

She takes a deep breath. "You gave a hooker money, Dragon."

"Yeah, but not for sex."

"But why?" She crosses her arms. "It could've been a sting operation. She could've been undercover."

"If she'd been an undercover cop, I'd be fine. Because I told her it wasn't for sex."

She chews on her bottom lip. I'm right and she knows it.

She lets out a sigh. "I'm thinking it might be better if you found somewhere else to live."

"Yeah, I figured you'd say that." I look down.

"You don't have to get out right away. But I think you should look."

"Who was that guy you were with?"

She furrows her brow. "Antonio? I told you. He's a friend."

Recognition dawns on me. "He was at the party."

"Yeah, he's actually Teddy's cousin. He owns a music store here in town."

My eyebrows nearly fly off my head. "Does he—"

"Before you say another word, yes, he employs instructors for vocal and instrumental music. But after tonight, I'm not so sure you're what he has in mind."

"I'm as good a drummer as anybody."

"I certainly wouldn't know."

"Ask Jesse. He always said I was better than any of the percussion performance majors he knew in school. And I'm completely self-taught."

"Dragon..."

"You know what?" I run my hands over my face and through my hair. "Never mind. Doesn't matter anyway. I'll be out of here as soon as I find another place to live."

I close the door in her face.

I head back toward my shower when she pounds on the door.

No knocking softly this time. She's pounding on it like her life depends on it.

I open the door. "Yes?"

Her hands are on her hips. "Damn it, Dragon. You will not close the door on me. You will not..."

She's yelling, her cheeks red, her hands balled into fists.

And all I can think about is that my life is a piece of shit, but here stands before me the most beautiful woman I've ever seen.

And she's full of fire I didn't know she had.

She's yammering about something, her lips flapping like a

hummingbird's wings, and all I want is for her to shut up.

So I shut her up the only way I can.

I crush my mouth to hers.

CHAPTER NINETEEN

DIANA

How is this man's tongue in my mouth?

He holds me tightly, and I grab his shoulders, try to wrench myself away from him.

But his kiss...

His kiss is giving me something I can't deny...

His tongue is velvet, his lips so soft and full, and he tastes of chocolate and cherries.

And of musk and spice and something that's uniquely him.

He tastes of a dragon.

I melt into him for a moment, explore his mouth with my own... Until—

I push harder against his chest, breaking the kiss. I wipe my lips with the back of my hand.

"What the hell was that?"

"Tell me you didn't enjoy it," he growls.

"Are you kidding me?"

"Say it, Diana." He brings a finger to my lip. "Say you didn't enjoy that kiss, and I'll be out of here by morning."

I gulp, sucking in a breath. My heart is beating so fast, I feel like it might pop right out of my chest.

My body is on fire, the heat culminating between my legs.

A shiver runs through me—so odd, the chill against the

heat.

My nipples are hard, and all I can think about...

All I can think about...

"I'm waiting. Say it. You want to get rid of me by morning? All you have to do is tell me you didn't enjoy that kiss."

I swallow. "I didn't enjoy that kiss."

But my voice cracks, and I have a hard time with the words.

"Very well." He moves to shut his door.

But I stick my bootie-clad foot in it.

His hazel eyes are on fire. "What is it?" he demands.

"You know very well what it is." I wag my finger at him. "Who do you think you are, kissing me like that?"

"You kissed me back, Diana."

He's not wrong, but I lie anyway. "I did not."

"My tongue may have been in your mouth, but yours was in mine as well." He narrows his eyes. "It was a phenomenal kiss, Diana. As phenomenal a kiss as I've ever experienced. Shame you didn't enjoy it."

Oh my God. I squeeze my thighs together, trying to ease the ache between them.

"Is there anything else?" he asks.

I open my mouth to reply, but only a soft sigh flows out of me.

And then I do something completely stupid, completely out of character, but it feels more right than anything I've done in a long time.

I grab his shoulders, pull him back into me, and mash our mouths together once more.

Our lips slide together, our teeth, gums, tongues.

All of it, all in this kiss.

Is it the two glasses of wine I drank? Is it my attraction to Antonio from earlier?

Or is it just Dragon?

Dragon... A man who affects me like no man ever has.

He groans into my mouth, and I feel it vibrate all the way to my toes.

He's a beast.

Not the kind of guy I'd ever go for...

But I crave the beast in him.

I crave the darkness in him.

I crave all of him.

He pulls me into his room, and in a moment my back is against the wall, and his hardness is grinding into my belly.

What does his dick look like?

I want to see his naked body, feel his rippling muscles. Untie his hair from its band and run my fingers through his long strands.

All the while he's devouring me with his kiss.

Eating me whole, and I welcome it.

I should stop this.

I know better.

He was just arrested for soliciting a prostitute, for God's sake.

But my body betrays my thoughts. I can't bring myself to care about any of that.

I want to dive into his darkness, embrace it, become part of him.

Sunlight is overrated.

We kiss and we kiss and we kiss. I wrap my arms around his neck. Sometime between leaving Teddy's and getting arrested, he put the band back in his hair.

I yank on it, pull it, not gently, and then I thread my fingers through his hair, its texture silky and soft, as I moan into his mouth, deepening the kiss.

He grinds his erection into me harder, and my God...

I'm pulsing.

I move my hands out of his hair, slide them over his shoulders, down his slim hips to his ass. I grab his butt cheeks, standing on my tiptoes so that my clit is hitting the hardness beneath his jeans.

Damn... How long has it been since I've had a climax?

Too long, as I'm ready to come right now from a good dry hump.

I grind into his groin, still tangling my tongue with his—

Until he's no longer kissing me.

He's a foot away from me, piercing me with those gold-flecked hazel eyes.

"Don't start something you're not going to finish," he snarls.

Chills skitter over my spine.

This is my get-out-of-jail-free card.

My chance to escape.

He'll be gone by morning—or so he says—and I'll never have to lay eyes on him again.

Until, of course, the band plays at one of my family's gatherings on the western slope.

Fuck.

I'll never be free of Dragon.

And what drives me even crazier?

At this moment, I don't want to be free of him.

"I'm waiting for your answer," he says, his voice low and husky.

I blink several times. "You didn't ask a question. You made a demand of me. You demanded that I not start something that I don't intend to finish." I close the distance between us so that there are no more than a few inches between our mouths. "I finish everything I start, Dragon. But *I* didn't start this. You did."

"That's where you're wrong," he growls. "I may have kissed you first, but I stopped. The second kiss? That was all you."

I can't deny his words. Can't deny them because they're the God's honest truth.

"So tell me, Diana," he continues. "What is it that you're looking for tonight? Are you horny? Did Antonio not fulfill your needs?"

Before I can stop myself, my hand flies up, and I slap him across the face.

"Antonio is a gentleman. We didn't do anything. I wasn't looking for..."

He meets my gaze, his cheek beginning to redden. "You're looking for what then, Diana? A breath-catching make-out session? Some long, slow, and languid lovemaking?" His face darkens. "Because if any of that is what you're looking for, you won't find it with me."

"Won't I?"

He runs a finger from my neck down to the tips of my thumb, nearly making me collapse to the floor. "I can only take you into hell, Diana. You won't get hearts and flowers from me."

I draw in a breath. "Maybe I don't want hearts and flowers."

"Are you sure you want a visit from an honest-to-God demon?"

I step backward, my breath pitching. My heart is already stampeding, but it nearly stops at his words.

He takes a step toward me, closing the distance between us. "Because that's what you'll get with me. I can satisfy you. I can make your body hum with desire." He takes another step. "But you won't get hearts and flowers. You won't get love, Diana." One final step. He's less than an inch away from me. "You'll only get lust and wrath...and a little bit of gluttony."

I raise an eyebrow. "What about sloth? Which other deadly sins are you ready to give me?"

"I don't have to give you any sins," he says. "Because I *am* sin, Diana. I am darkness. I live in hell on earth, and that's where I'll take you."

Goose bumps take over my flesh until I'm convinced I'm an icicle. An icicle with a heated core.

Do I really think Dragon is hell on earth?

No.

But do I think *he* thinks it?

He must, or why would he say it?

I'm not looking for love. But I'm not looking for hell, either.

I don't think he *is* hell.

But what I crave now is a little bit of his darkness.

If I have to go to hell to get it?

I'm ready to go.

Like I said, sunlight can be overrated.

You get too much of that? You crave a little darkness.

Dragon has darkness in abundance.

What if this isn't me?

What if my craving for a little bit of his darkness sends me into a spiral I don't want?

Diana's a good girl.

Diana always does the right thing.

Diana would never follow a rock star to Europe like her baby sister did.

Of course, Brianna ended up getting her heart's desire after taking the risk and leaping without a net.

But Dragon isn't my heart's desire.

I don't know what that is.

All I know is this moment.

And in this moment? I want Dragon Locke more than I've ever wanted any man in my lifetime.

"Well?" he asks, his voice low.

"Give me a minute."

"How many minutes do you need? Because I learned a long time ago to live for the day. For the minute. The goddamned second." He places his hand around my waist and draws my body against his. "Because your life can be over in an instant."

I part my lips, stop my jaw from dropping.

He's an addict, yes. He's had a rough night, getting arrested for something he claims he didn't do.

He's not talking about either of those things.

No. He's talking about something else entirely.

Something inside him—something that gives him his darkness.

I clear my throat, will my voice not to stammer. "I don't believe that you're hell. That you're sin."

The gold flecks in his eyes are almost glowing, perhaps with the fire and brimstone within him.

"Then you'd be wrong."

I set my hands on my hips. "Maybe I want a little darkness

in my life."

"A little darkness is one thing, Diana. I'm a whole other thing."

"I'm not sure what to say."

"If you think you've been a good girl all your life, and you think taking a man with a little bit of an edge to bed will be some kind of *experience*, then you're like a lot of women I've known." He grips my waist, his nails digging into my flesh through my sweater. "But let me make one thing abundantly clear. If that's what you're looking for? Look elsewhere. Because you can't even begin to know where I will take you."

I gulp. "The only person who believes you're that dark inside, Dragon, is you."

"I'm done talking." He advances toward me. "I want you. I want to sink my cock inside your sweet little cunt more than I want my next breath of air. But I won't force you. I may be sin, but I have my limits."

I breathe out sharply. "Then I'm right. You're *not* darkness personified."

He raises an eyebrow. "You think because I'm not a rapist I'm not dark? Think again, sweet girl. I can and *will* take you to hell."

I shrug then, my body on fire. "Do it, then. You think you've been to hell and back? Take me there, and then I'll tell you how dark you truly are."

CHAPTER TWENTY

DRAGON

My God, she's tempting.

I haven't been this tempted by a woman in a long time.

And I know damned well I need to leave my hands off her.

But there she stands, her dark eyes blazing, glaring at me, daring me.

Fucking *challenging* me to take her. To take her to hell.

She has no idea what I can do.

Getting involved with me will only drag her down.

As much as I want her—and even though she's basically offering herself up on a platter—I need to be the stronger person here. I need to think of her as a narcotic that I'm dying to get into my system.

And damn, I want her more than I've ever wanted any drug.

But I need to say no.

I need to be a better person.

I won't drag her sweet sunlight into my spiral of darkness.

She may want it. Hell, she may *need* it.

But she'll have to find it somewhere else.

I release my grip on her and take a step back. "Go to bed, Diana."

Her gorgeous eyes widen. "You're kidding, right?"

I shake my head. "I don't kid. How often have you seen me smile, Diana? How often have you heard me offer thanks when I know I should? How often have you seen me express anything other than darkness and negativity?"

"Prove it," she says.

"Prove what?"

She crosses her arms. "That you can take me to hell."

"You don't want me to prove that."

She takes a step toward me. "Yeah, I do. Because I'm not going to deny it anymore, Dragon. I'm horny as hell for you right now. I want to feel your naked body next to mine. I want to feel you inside me. And my guess is it will be more like heaven than hell."

My cock stretches farther.

Does she have a clue what she's doing to me?

I could fuck her into next week, and yeah, I could give her orgasm after orgasm, take her to the highest peaks in Colorado.

None of that changes the fact that I am sin. That I'm hell. It all might feel good while it's happening, but she'll regret it soon afterward.

I turn away from her. "I'm not a robot, Diana. I'm a flesh and blood man. My cock is as hard as it's ever been right now, so you need to shut the fuck up. You need to leave my room. I will pack up and be gone in the morning."

"So that's it?" She walks around me to face me. "You're all talk and no action?"

I shove my hands into my pockets. "You have no idea what you're talking about. No idea what you're asking me to do to you."

"Do you need me to spell it out for you?" She raises her hands to either side of her body. "I'm asking you to fuck me,

Dragon. Do you want me to unzip my jeans and prove to you how wet I am for you?"

I lean against my wall. My legs are unsteady. She's driving me to the brink of insanity, and if she doesn't stop, I *will* take her. I'll do what she's allowing me to do, and we'll both regret it.

I can't let that happen.

This is Jesse's sister-in-law. This is Diana Steel. A Steel heiress.

I grab her hand, lead her to the door, and then shove her through the doorframe. I close the door, locking it.

"Open back up!" She pounds on my door.

I throw my hands over my ears in an attempt to muffle her shouts. "Go to bed, Diana."

"You're a coward, Dragon. That's what you are. You're afraid of me."

I can't help a chuckle at that. "Diana, I'm not afraid of anything."

"Yes, you are. You're afraid I'm going to see through you. I'm going to see you're not what you claim to be."

"Go to bed. Use a vibrator on that wet pussy of yours. That's all I can offer you tonight."

She pounds again and again.

But eventually she stops, and I sit down on my bed, pull out my cock to ease the ache inside me.

I should get a fucking prize for this. She offered herself and her beautiful body, mine for the taking, and I let her go.

Maybe I'm not the ultimate darkness after all.

⁓

I sleep for a few hours, but by seven a.m. I'm awake and

packing my things, which takes all of about ten minutes. Diana's probably not up yet. At least I hope she's not. I want to simply leave the keys on the counter and go. Spare us both an embarrassing goodbye.

Where? I have no idea.

Maybe I'll call Jake and see if I can crash with him for a few days. I don't have a car, but I have enough money to catch a bus back to the western slope.

Of course, if I go back west, I'll no longer be close to my rehab facility, but I can call Tim anytime. He can talk me off any ledges I find myself on. I'll be back soon for my arraignment anyway.

I grab my duffel bag and my backpack, open the door to my bedroom, and walk out.

Only to drop my jaw when I get to the living room.

Diana's there, and fuck it all.

She's wearing a bright-red lace nightie that leaves nothing to the imagination.

Already my cock is responding.

She looks up at me. "Where are you going?"

"I told you I'd be out by morning."

She walks up to me and grabs my hand. Sparks shoot through my body.

"Dragon, don't leave. We both know you need to be here."

I look her up and down. "Why are you dressed like that?"

"This is what I sleep in." Her cheeks turn pink. "You think I put this on for you?"

It was a little presumptuous of me, I suppose. Maybe she *does* sleep in lace nighties. I can see the outline of her nipples. At least she's wearing panties. If I could see that bare pussy, God...

"I just want to apologize," she says. "I..."

"You what?"

She lets out a forced chuckle. "I was going to apologize for throwing myself at you. But then I realized I'm not sorry. I mean, you started it with that kiss."

"I kissed you to get you to shut up," I say.

She cocks her head. "You did?"

"Yeah, I did. You were yammering on and on about how I got myself into trouble last night." I cross my arms. "You don't even believe me, do you? You think I was actually soliciting that poor girl?"

Her shoulders slump, and she doesn't respond.

"Then why didn't you believe me when I told you I was sin? That I would take you to hell? You clearly believe the worst of me, Diana, and there's nothing I can do to change that."

She takes a deep breath, tenting her fingers in front of her chest. "I thought a lot about it. We were both in a weird place last night, and it's probably best that we didn't...you know."

I simply nod.

Jacking off got me the release I needed, but damn, standing here looking at her... I still want her more than anything.

"Agreed." I take a step toward the door. "Now if you'll excuse me, I'll get out of your hair."

She stands then, walks to me, and my gaze falls to her beautiful legs.

"Stay. Please. We'll make this work. I start my new job tomorrow anyway, and I won't be home much. Besides, we need to find you a lawyer."

"Last I checked, that's my problem, not yours."

She wrinkles her nose. "I have contacts. My brother's on

his honeymoon, of course, and my mother's retired, but do you think they're the only two lawyers I know?"

"I can't imagine your mother or your brother would represent me anyway."

"They would if I asked them to. But I don't have to ask them. You need a criminal defense attorney, and neither of them practice that kind of law."

"I suppose you know someone who does?"

"Not personally, but I know lawyers, and I can get you a referral."

"I can't afford any kind of lawyer that you recommend."

She stomps her foot. "For God's sake, Dragon, I'm not saying you'll have to pay for it. There are people who owe me favors. Who owe my family favors. Why can't you get that through your thick head?"

I sigh. "Because I'm done taking from your family, Diana. That's why I can't live here."

"God, you sound just like Jesse." She rolls her eyes. "Don't take Steel money. Don't you know by now that we have enough to last a hundred lifetimes?"

"Doesn't mean I'm entitled to any of it."

"No, it doesn't mean that. And quite frankly, it doesn't mean I'm entitled to any of it either. I just happened to be born into this family. You think I did anything to earn a penny of it?"

I stop a moment, gaze at her. The look on her face is serious. She believes what she's saying. And she's right, of course. Most of the Steel fortune was made before she was even born.

"It'll be easier for me to help you if you're here." She steps in front of the door. "So don't go. Accept my apology and stay here."

I should apologize to her as well. I had no right to kiss her the way I did or say anything about the guy she was with—and she had every right to slap me.

"Do you think we'll be able to resist these urges we both seem to have?" I ask her.

She chuckles nervously. "We're adults. I think we can certainly exercise a modicum of self-control."

Her nipples are hard. Poking through that lace.

And it's not because it's cold in here.

My dick is so hard, stretching my jeans.

When her gaze drops, I know she sees it too.

And that just makes it harder.

She walks toward me.

She touches my forearm.

And I burn.

How did it come to this?

I should've fucked her last night. Maybe I would've gotten it out of my system.

Maybe that's what we both need.

So I grab her, pull her into me, and kiss her hard.

She opens for me, and her tongue twirls with mine. It's not as frantic as it was last night, but it's full of passion and desire.

She doesn't back away.

She doesn't fear what I can do to her.

She doesn't fear hell.

My breath catches as she slides her warm fingers underneath my T-shirt. When she gets to my nipple, she jerks away.

"Never felt a pierced nipple before?" I ask after breaking the kiss.

She doesn't reply. Instead, she shoves my jacket over my

shoulders, and it falls to the floor. Then she pulls my T-shirt up, exposing my chest and pierced nipples.

She sucks in a breath. "Oh my God."

I'm not sure what to say to that. I've had this tattoo for over ten years. It took five different sessions with the artist. Soaring across my chest is a glittering gold-and-green dragon, with touches of red on the tail and the eyes.

My nipple rings are simple silver bars.

She traces the dragon with her fingers, and when her fingernails scrape over my nipples, they harden further.

"Who did this?" she asks.

"A guy in Barrel Oaks."

"Not Cy in Snow Creek?"

"Nope. A guy who works out of his home over in Barrel Oaks. I did some handyman work for him one time, and this is how he paid me."

"Amazing." She takes a step back and takes the whole thing in. "I've never seen anything like it."

My guess is she's never seen any man with his entire chest tattooed.

But I don't say that.

"How did I not know about this?" she asks.

I shrug. "It doesn't really come up in conversation. Anybody ask you about your tattoos?"

She bites her lip. "I don't have any."

I smirk. "There you go."

She takes a step forward and wraps her hands around my waist. "I guess I've never seen you without a shirt. Never at a pool or anything."

"We don't exactly run in the same circles, Diana."

She twists her lips into a frown, and God, she's still

beautiful. "I didn't mean to imply—"

I shake my head. "Of course you didn't. No offense taken. I haven't exactly been invited to any Steel pool parties. The only time I'm at your place is when the band performs."

"Do you have any other work?"

"No."

It's a lie, of course. I have a griffin on the back of my thigh, in a place I can't see it. But I know it's there.

She doesn't ask about the meaning of the dragon. Why should she? It's my name, so it's pretty self-explanatory.

But if I tell her about the griffin, she'll ask why. That's not a story I'm ready to tell.

Especially not to Diana Steel.

I'm about ready to open my mouth and tell her I need to go now when—

I groan when she flicks her tongue over one of my nipples.

"God," I growl.

"I've never seen a man with pierced nipples before." She slides her tongue over the other one. "In pictures, of course, but never in real life."

I tremble at the touch of her tongue. "You need to stop that."

She looks up, her eyebrows raised. "What if I don't want to?"

"You think I want you to?"

"No, I don't. It's pretty clear how hard you are right now, Dragon." She slides her hand down to my bulge and squeezes.

I gasp in a breath. "You need to stop that," I say again.

"That's not what you want."

"How the hell would you ever know what I want?"

"This massive erection you have isn't for your health,

Dragon. You want me as much as *I* want you."

I open my mouth to speak, but she slides two fingers over my lips.

"I'm not saying any of this makes sense. Do you think I thought for a minute I would end up wanting you like this? And I'm hardly *your* type either."

"Yeah," I scoff. "Beautiful, long legs, gorgeous tits, and red lace sure isn't my type."

She huffs. "You know what I mean. I imagine you're attracted to those blue-haired women with tattoos all over their bodies."

A lot she knows about me. I hate blue hair. I hate any unnatural color of hair. I mean, do what you want, but it's not something I like. Diana has a cousin named Ava who has pink hair. She's a beautiful woman, but the hair does nothing for me.

And as for tattoos? I like them when they're tasteful. My whole chest may be covered with one, but I'd never cover my whole body. I don't think it looks good when others do.

I slide her hand away from my crotch. "We've been through this."

"I know. Doesn't change the fact that I want you. And you clearly feel the same way."

I swallow. "Sometimes what we want isn't good for us."

"Oh, I know." She licks her bottom lip.

I grow even harder.

"I'm not just talking about you, Diana. I won't be good for you, but you won't be good for *me* either."

She lifts her eyebrows.

"What? You never stopped to think about that? Every coin has two sides, Diana. I'll ruin you, and you'll ruin *me* right back."

She blinks. "How could I possibly ruin anyone?" she asks, her voice dripping with innocence.

I chuckle. "People like you never see it. You live life with a silver spoon in your mouth. You don't know what the real world is like."

Her eyes narrow. "That's where you're wrong, Dragon. You know what my family's been through."

I nod slowly. "I know some of it. And finding out your family used to be involved in human trafficking is horrific, I won't deny that. But you didn't live it, Diana. It didn't happen to you."

She gulps then, audibly, and tears well in her eyes. "Not to me, but to my brothers and my father."

This time I widen my eyes.

She turns her head away, wiping her eyes. "I can see that's news to you."

"Fuck," is all I can say.

"It's not something we talk about." She grabs a tissue and dabs her eyes. "In fact, it's not something I even knew until a year ago. But our family isn't all riches and light, Dragon. We have our dark secrets too, and they might be just as dark as yours."

"Maybe," I say. "Maybe not. But you'll never know because there are some things I never talk about."

She takes a step toward me again. "Would you like to?"

"Hell no."

"If you want to talk, I'll be happy to listen. I will hold every word you say to me in confidence. And if you don't want to talk?" She stands on her tiptoes and brushes her soft lips against mine. "I can help you with that, too."

CHAPTER TWENTY-ONE

DIANA

He parts his lips and shoves his tongue between mine.

Another kiss, and it's perfection.

Yes, it's dark, and yes, it's Dragon, but I wouldn't want it any other way.

I'm curious about his background—everyone is—but right now, I can be content just to kiss him.

Maybe let him take me to bed.

Perhaps I'll take *him* to bed.

What the hell am I thinking?

Except for once, I don't want to think.

I've spent my life thinking, being the good girl.

Keeping myself out of trouble after trouble found me— naïve, unsuspecting me—freshman year at that homecoming bonfire.

No, not now.

No more thinking.

For once I'm going to *do* without thinking.

And right now, this is the best kiss I've ever had.

Dragon is a dragon. I swear he's breathing fire into me. My entire body is hot, molten.

How long has it been since I've been with a man? Too damned long.

I break the kiss with a loud pop.

His eyes are narrowed, smoldering in their intensity.

"Are you sure?" he says, his voice cracking.

I nod.

"You'd better be damned sure, Diana. Because once we start this, we're going to finish."

I nod again.

"Say it. Say the words, Diana."

"The words, Diana." I smile.

He pushes me against the wall, not gently. "Damn it. This isn't a game. If that's what you think it is, I won't play." He scowls. "I don't play games with women. I don't play games with *anyone*, for that matter. But I sure as hell don't play games with women I want to take into my bed. If you're not all in, this isn't happening."

My God, he's angry. And I can't blame him. Why did I decide to joke around at that time? Bad timing on my part for sure.

"Dragon, I—"

He claps his hand over my mouth. "Stop right there. The only words I want to hear from that succulent little mouth of yours are, 'Dragon, take me to bed and fuck me.'"

It's funny. I grew up with two brothers and a potty-mouth sister, but I don't often use those words.

Still, as they come out of Dragon's mouth, they send jolts of electricity all through me.

He removes his hand from my mouth. "What do you want to say, Diana?"

I open my mouth, ready to say what he wants to hear.

But nothing comes out.

He nods. "Just as I thought."

He turns.

Oh my God, he's going to leave.

And I may never see him again.

Except that's not true.

My sister's married to the lead singer of his rock band. Of course I'll see him again. I'll probably see him more often than I see most men.

"Don't," I say.

He looks up at me, meets my gaze. "Don't what?"

I open my mouth to tell him not to leave, but different words altogether come out.

"Take me to bed, Dragon. Take me to bed and fuck me."

I expect him to come toward me, ask me if I'm sure.

But he doesn't.

Instead, he lifts me into his arms as if I weigh no more than a feather. A moment later we're in his bedroom, on his bed, our mouths fused together.

I'd rather be in my own bedroom, but this is better. Even though it's my place, this is his sacred space. Not my own. I'm not quite ready to give him my space yet.

But I'm ready to give him pretty much anything else he wants.

He rips his mouth from mine and looks down at me, his hazel eyes on fire. "This won't be pretty, Diana. It won't be gentle. It may hurt."

"I can take it," I say.

"This isn't going to be a sweet and gentle fuck like you're used to."

I narrow my gaze. "Who says I'm used to sweet and gentle?"

He furrows his brow. "It's written all over your face. All

over your demeanor. It's written all over you, Diana."

He's not wrong.

I'm experienced with sex. I'm nearly twenty-six years old, and I've had many boyfriends. But he's right. It's always been kind of...ordinary.

Not that I didn't enjoy it. I could always have an orgasm, but there was always something missing.

I've never experienced that all-consuming passion—that fire, that sense of urgency—that I'm experiencing right now.

Right now, with a man I never thought I'd be attracted to.

But Dragon fills up the room.

Not the way my brothers fill a room with their sheer handsomeness and presence.

No, Dragon fills up the room in a different way.

He fills it with darkness, with seductive sin, with a desire to fill my needs in the dark of night.

"I don't do things I don't want to do," I say.

"Neither do I. It's no secret that I want to shove my cock in you and fuck you into next week. That's all I can offer you right now, Diana. If you want me to leave after that, I'll leave."

"You don't have to leave."

"Are you not hearing me? I'm not offering you a relationship. I'm not even offering you a date."

"Did I ask for one?"

"Jesus Christ." He crushes his mouth to mine once more.

If possible, the kiss is even more urgent this time. He pushes his tongue into my mouth with the force of a hurricane.

Where is Diana? Sweet smart Diana who used to think most men used too much tongue?

Because damn it, Dragon is using more than enough. Yet I'm craving more.

I wish I could open up my skin and let him crawl into me.

We kiss for several minutes until he breaks it, rolling over and gasping in a deep breath.

I need a breath myself. I'm panting, sweat erupting on my hairline.

"God, you look sexy in that thing," Dragon says. "I'd like to rip it off you until it's in shreds."

"No one is stopping you."

"I suppose not." He cocks his head. "You can buy ten more tomorrow."

Christ. "You don't need to keep reminding me of how different we are," I say. "No one knows that more than I do. But right now, we're just two people. Two horny people who really want each other. You've made it clear you're not promising anything past this. I'm not either. Tomorrow I start a job that will take up most of my time. I'll hardly be home. It's part of why I went to that party last night. I'm not a big partier. I wanted a last hurrah."

"And that's what I am?"

I open my mouth to tell him yes, it is, but something stops me.

I don't want to think of this as a last hurrah.

This is something in a category of its own. I'm just not sure what category it is yet.

"And if you are?" I ask.

"Works for me."

His T-shirt is already off, and I can't help gaping at the gorgeous tattoo on his chest. At the sexy nipple rings.

"Maybe *I* should get nipple rings," I say as I peel my nightie off my body, letting my breasts fall gently against my chest.

"Fuck no." He stares at my tits. "Don't do anything to them. They're perfect just as they are."

My nipples harden further at his words. They're already so hard, I feel like they're going to pop off.

"Fuck," he growls as he leans toward me, cups both of them, and then moves downward to take one nipple between his lips.

Sparks fly through me, and every nerve inside me is dancing under my skin.

It all culminates in my pussy, already throbbing to the beat of my racing heart.

God... I've never been this horny this quickly. I'm near orgasm already, and he hasn't even touched me between my legs.

I close my eyes, moan softly, as he sucks my nipple more gently than I expect.

But not for long.

He twists the other one between his fingers to the point of a feeling so intense that I cry out, but in pleasure, not pain.

"Yeah, you like that?" he murmurs against my breast.

"God, yes."

"Damn, you're gorgeous. I've never seen tits this great. I could suck on them all night."

"Except it's morning..." I say softly.

"All the better," he says. He sucks harder on the nipple, lets go of the other and massages it before he twists it again.

I suck in a breath, gasping.

"Fuck, your tits are responsive."

They always have been, but they respond to Dragon like they've never responded before.

"You like it a little rough, don't you?"

I'm not sure how to answer that. I never thought I would, but apparently I do.

I move my hips absently, searching, searching, searching...

Until he finally slides one hand inside my panties.

Then a groan so guttural, I feel like the earth has moved under us.

"Fuck, you're wet. So wet."

I move against his finger as he slides it through my folds. Subliminally I'm telling him to put one inside me, to ease the ache of emptiness.

As if reading my mind, he shoves not one but two inside my heat.

And that's all it takes.

I stumble over the precipice and into a climax so intense, I actually see stars.

CHAPTER TWENTY-TWO

DRAGON

"Fuck, you're hot," I say through gritted teeth.

Her pussy walls are clamping around my fingers, and all I can think about is how they're going to feel against my cock.

When her climax calms down a little, I take my fingers out of her pussy and put them in my mouth, licking her juices.

Damn...

She's sweeter than cream. I still have my cock encased in my jeans.

But I can't help myself. That orgasm from her turned me on so much that I climb on top of her, slide my still-encased cock against her clit, and move.

"Oh my God." She shudders beneath me.

"You like that?"

"God... I feel... I feel..."

I grind against her, all the while thinking of how perfect she's going to feel around me, but I need to see her come again.

I need to know that *I'm* the one making her come.

"Feel how much I want you," I growl. "I'm hard as a rock inside these jeans. Do you feel that? Do you feel it, Diana? How much I fucking want you?"

"Dragon"—she bites her lip—"please..."

"Please what? Please fuck you? Please take my cock out

of my jeans and fuck you until you're bleeding?"

She opens her eyes wider when I mention bleeding, but then her cheeks redden, and she closes her eyes with a sigh.

"Yes. Please."

I roll off her then, slide her panties off, and then move to the side of the bed where I ditch my shoes and socks, unbuckle my jeans, slide them and my boxer briefs over my hips and leave them on the floor.

I give my cock a few quick pulls to ease the ache.

Doesn't help.

Not that I thought it would.

I grab a condom out of my pocket, rip it open, and quickly sheath myself.

I'm ready.

Ready to fuck her.

But when I turn, see her flushed body lying on the bed, her legs spread seductively, her nipples red and ruddy from my attention and still pebbled hard, all I can do for a moment is simply look at the beauty before me.

I've been with good-looking women before.

Hell, I've been with beautiful women before.

Diana's in a class all her own.

She's perfectly put together. Shorter than her sister, but still tall enough. Perfect breasts, which she obviously got from her mother.

A gorgeous shaved pussy, and then of course between her legs...

That pink swollen paradise that I can't wait to dive into.

She was so sweet when I licked her from my fingers. I want to eat her. Want to fucking dive my tongue inside her heat and eat her all damned day.

But I have to get into her first. Sink my hard cock into her. I need to release.

God, I need to release.

Last night was so...so...

I stop thinking. I hover over her for a split second, and then I thrust into her.

She gasps, her eyes widening.

"Okay?" I ask.

"Yes. I feel so..."

"Full?"

She closes her eyes. "Full in the best way. Complete."

Her word choice startles me. This is a onetime thing, but I can't disagree with the truth of what she just said. I feel complete as well. I stay inside, embedded in her, for a moment before my cock tells me it's time to go.

I pull out and thrust back in.

God, she's even tighter this time. I grunt and groan as I fuck her.

I told her it would be a hard and fast fuck, and I wasn't lying.

Thrust, thrust, thrust...

Already my balls are tingling, scrunching, ready to release.

I stay inside her for a brief time, cooling myself off. As much as I need to come, I need to feel her pussy around me more.

I shiver when she wraps her legs around my hips and then grabs my ass, pushing me with my own rhythm.

"You like to be fucked, Diana? You like to be fucked with my big hard cock?"

She sighs beneath me, biting her lip, nodding.

"Then open your eyes. Look into mine. I'm going to make

you come, and I want your eyes open when you do."

She pops her eyes open, her cheeks flushed a gorgeous pink.

"I want us to come together. Are you ready to come again?"

She nods. "Almost there, Dragon." She nibbles on her lip again. "Almost there."

I plunge into her a few more times, as deeply as I can, so that I know my pubic bone is hitting her clit.

She groans with each plunge, until—

"Yes! I'm coming again. Again..."

I pull back out one more time and shove myself so hard into her, releasing.

Electric sparks shoot through my balls all the way through my dick and into Diana.

When she comes, she milks me, prolonging my orgasm.

And I swear to God...

Swear to fucking God...

It's the best climax of my life.

I've completely gone over the edge, and when the pulses finally subside, I realize that my eyes are closed. That I didn't look into her eyes as we came together.

I missed it.

I missed the connection.

It shouldn't bother me, but it does.

That only means one thing.

I promised her only today... But we're going to do this again.

Because I need to see Diana's eyes as we come together.

I need that more than I've needed anything in a long time.

CHAPTER TWENTY-THREE

DIANA

I can't even think right now.

The sweet pink haze of my orgasm surrounds me, and I feel like I'm imploding inside a cloud.

Dragon's eyes are closed, but as I look at his face, I see something.

Is it a bit of light in his usual darkness?

A bit of peace in his usual chaos?

If I could do that for him, this was time well spent.

But it wasn't altruistic on my part.

My God, I wanted this. I wanted it more than I've ever wanted anything in my life. More than the dream job I start tomorrow, which until last night was the only thing I truly cared about.

And that is a scary thing indeed.

He doesn't make any move to pull out, so I keep my legs wrapped around him, slide my hands up his back, massage small circles into his shoulders.

For a moment—a blissful moment—I imagine that we're together. That he wasn't arrested for solicitation last night. That we're something more than roommates.

We're different as night and day, so that will never happen.

There's certainly no future for Dragon and me.

Besides, I got what I was after.

I let myself dive into his darkness, and now that it's over, I find I'm not gasping for air.

Instead...I'm craving more.

We stay joined for several more minutes, until finally Dragon opens his eyes and pulls out. He moves to the side of the bed and disposes of his condom, and then he slides back next to me.

"Did you get what you need?" I ask.

"For now," he says.

He rolls over onto his side, his back to me.

I can't help but stare. His shoulders and back are rippled, so sexy, and his firm ass is as gorgeous as I knew it would be.

And his thighs—

I lift my eyebrows in surprise. Dragon has another tattoo on the back of his thigh. He said he didn't have any other work, but he lied. It's some kind of creature with the body of a lion and the head and wings of an eagle.

I absently trace the lines of the image with my fingers, and he jerks away from my touch.

A moment later, he's facing me.

"What happened?" I ask. "You don't want me touching you?"

He frowns. "Just not there."

"Why? I just wanted to see your tattoo. You said you didn't have any others." I sit up and peer over to the other side of his thigh. "What is it?"

He slaps his hand down over it, blocking my view. "It's a griffin. And that's all I'm saying."

A griffin. Yes. I recognize it now. I swallow. "Okay. I didn't mean to upset you."

"You didn't." He kisses my cheek. "You done coming?"

"I..."

"Because if you're not, I'm going to spread those gorgeous legs of yours and eat you until you scream."

There's no woman alive who doesn't love receiving oral sex, and I'm no exception.

"I won't turn that down."

"Good," he growls. "I wasn't planning to ask for permission."

He crawls between my legs, spreads them, and for a moment just looks at me. "Beautiful," he growls.

Then his tongue is on me, licking me, his teeth nibbling on my clit, still sensitive from the last orgasm.

God, he was right.

It's not gentle.

He nibbles on my thighs, tugs on my labia, slides his whole tongue into my pussy.

It's like he's been starving on a desert island for weeks and I'm an all-you-can-eat buffet.

He moans and groans for me, and I lift my hips, grinding against his stubble.

It won't take long for me to come again.

I move my hips, sliding my sensitive tissues against his face, following his movements, letting his stubble graze me, burn me.

He uses his fingers then, sliding them against my thighs, over my ass, squeezing my cheeks.

And then—

"Oh!"

He breaches the rim of my asshole with a finger—a finger wet with my pussy juices.

He raises his eyebrows at me from between his legs.

This is it.

I can tell him to stop.

But I don't.

I don't want to stop.

No man has ever gone there before, and while I can't say I'm ready for his cock down there—he's huge, after all— this is something new, and I want to experience it. I want to experience it with Dragon.

The feeling is odd and probe-like at first, but as he continues to suck on my pussy lips, the invasion grows on me.

It's so forbidden—so taboo—and damn if it's not arousing as hell.

He sucks on my clit, harder and harder, as I grind against him, relish this new invasion of my body.

In a moment—

"God!" I thread my fingers through his long hair as I come against his face.

He continues to pump his finger in and out of my ass, adding to the rhythm of my climax.

And I'll be damned if it's not the most explosive climax I've ever experienced.

It goes on and on and on, and Dragon shows no sign of stopping.

Until finally—

I let go of his hair, go limp against the bed.

I'm drained.

So drained.

So relaxed.

Enveloped in a cloud of hazy euphoria.

When the orgasm finally subsides, Dragon is next to me,

and when I open my eyes, he's staring straight down at me.

I'm not sure what to say.

I'm not embarrassed, exactly. But...I feel odd. I shouldn't. We've just seen each other at our most vulnerable. We've just given each other incredible pleasure.

Finally, I swallow. "Why are you staring at me like that?"

He takes a deep breath in and lets it out on a sigh. "Because there's nothing more beautiful than a woman who's just had an amazing fuck."

I can't help myself. My lips curve slightly upward. "And I suppose you see a lot of them."

He shrugs. "I've seen my share, but I've never seen one so beautiful as you are, Diana."

My skin prickles through my orgasmic haze.

His words.

Just words.

Just words in his low voice, his dark demeanor.

They soak into me as if I'm lying in a warm bath being infused with aromatic oils.

I can't deny I wanted this.

But where does it leave us now?

Will he leave? Will he stay? How do I feel about either of those options?

When he finally breaks his gaze away from mine, I instinctively roll over onto my side away from him.

I like his eyes. I like that he's looking at me. I like that he gets pleasure from doing so.

But I have to stop.

Because if I don't...I could get hypnotized by Dragon's eyes.

And I might be lost forever.

CHAPTER TWENTY-FOUR

DRAGON

Man, she was a hot little fuck.

That tight little cunt of hers clenched around me like no one ever has, and that asshole...

God, how I'd love to get in there.

She turned away from me, and just as well.

We're in my room.

Except it's not my room. It's her room. This is her place.

She told me I didn't have to leave, but I feel like I should.

Where the hell would I go, though?

I'm rapidly running out of money, and until the band gets back in gear, I don't have any way to make a living.

Today is Sunday. I could go out and start looking for a job, but who the hell is hiring on a Sunday?

I honestly didn't mean for this to happen. I was ready to grab a bus back to the western slope, hit up Jake and Cage for a place to crash.

But now...

Fuck.

I really didn't mean...

Not that I didn't enjoy it. She's the best fuck I ever had.

I'm not sure I've ever wanted a woman quite so badly as I wanted her last night. And then this morning.

I roll over, sit on the edge of the bed.

My dick is hardening again.

I could have her again. I'll be hard as a rock in a minute just thinking about her. Just thinking about how those walls feel around me. How her tightness clamped around my finger.

I need to get out of here, though.

My stuff is still packed, and I need to think.

To figure out how to get out of this whole soliciting thing.

Normally, when I'm in trouble, I call Jesse. But I'm not going to bother him on his honeymoon. I've caused him enough trouble the past several months.

Sunday. A day with nothing to do. A day where neither of us will leave the apartment.

That's it.

I'm leaving.

I rise, head to my bathroom. Turn on the shower.

I already showered once this morning, before I packed up to leave, and though I hate the idea of rinsing Diana from me, I feel like a shower's the right choice.

I'm kind of hoping she'll join me, but already I know she won't.

And that's okay too.

I won't fall in love with her.

I don't fall in love. I've never been in love.

Hell, I don't even know what love is.

I used to love my parents. Used to love Griffin.

But then my parents abandoned me.

And Griffin disappeared.

Bad things happen to the people I love. Or they do bad things to me.

I've talked a lot to the therapist about that. I've always

known I can't blame Griffin. She was only five years old.

I wish she had told my parents that I wasn't the one who hurt her.

I wish a lot of things.

Because whoever hurt her that time came back.

They came back and they took her.

But I was gone by then, so I couldn't protect her.

Forced into the system by my own parents who thought I was a threat to their little girl.

They never knew what I really felt about Griffin. Like she was a little angel—light to my darkness.

I never would've hurt her.

In fact, I—

No. I shake my head, letting the water drizzle over me. No more thinking about that shit right now. I turn up the temperature on the water, get a rush from the scalding heat.

That's how I like my showers—scalding. That's another thing I've talked to my therapist about. My need to constantly cleanse the bad stuff from me.

The problem is? It can't be done. Hot showers feel good. But afterward, nothing really changes.

I clean my body, shampoo my long hair, and rinse off.

As I expected, Diana doesn't join me, and also as I expected, when I leave the bathroom...

She's gone.

We don't have to talk about what happened between us. Just as well, because I have no more desire to do that than I'm sure she does.

What can I say? I told her what would happen. I told her I'd give her a good hard fuck, that I'd take her to hell.

She let me do it.

I gave her several outs. She didn't take any of them.

What's done is done, and I can't bring myself to regret it.

How can I regret something that was one of the most spectacular experiences of my life?

I'm a guy. Consequently I love fucking.

But what Diana and I shared went so far beyond that. I won't use some stupid euphemism like making love. I can only say that she took me to a place I've never been.

And it wasn't hell.

It was a place I'd like to revisit.

But a place I'll probably have to let live in my memory.

I get dressed quickly in jeans and a black button-down shirt. The sun is shining, of course, as it usually does in Colorado. I have no idea where I'm going, but I need to get something to eat.

What the hell? I bought groceries yesterday. I should eat here because the money's already been spent.

My stuff is still packed. If Diana wants me to leave, I will. But not before I sample some of the groceries I paid for.

I walk out, looking to the right and then to the left. The door to Diana's bedroom is closed, so I assume she's in there. I don't hear the shower running, but why would I? She has a huge en suite bathroom, and I probably can't hear anything from here. I head into the kitchen and open the refrigerator. I take out the loaf of bread I bought plus a package of Black Forest ham and Colby-Jack cheese.

I bring all my ingredients over to the counter, search through the drawers until I find a plate, and assemble my sandwich. I grab a glass, get some water from the refrigerator door, and sit down on one of the barstools in front of the granite island.

I look over my shoulder toward Diana's room.

The door is still closed.

My guess is she won't come out until I'm gone. Or at least back in my room.

Is she embarrassed? Sorry that we did what we did?

I'm neither.

But I admit I'm not sure what I need to say to her.

I take a bite of my sandwich. It's palatable, but I'd rather be at the diner.

I like hot food.

All those years in the group home, the hot food was lukewarm if even that. It was about the same at the rehab facility.

I finish my sandwich quickly, and then I leave.

But I'll be back.

I didn't bring the bags that I packed. They're still safely in my room.

CHAPTER TWENTY-FIVE

DIANA

"But you said the two of you weren't together," Teddy says through my phone after I spill my guts about what happened with Dragon this morning.

"We're not." I swallow. "I'm not exactly sure how it happened, but now he's here, and I don't know what to do."

"Fuck his brains out again?" Teddy chuckles.

I scoff. "God, I can't do that."

"Why not, Diana? You're starting work at that new job first thing in the morning. When the hell else are you going to have a chance to take care of yourself? Of your *needs*?"

"It's just... He's got a lot of baggage, you know?"

"What kind of baggage?"

I look out the door of my bedroom to make sure that Dragon isn't within earshot and then lower my voice. "No one really knows, other than his addiction. But there's a big story there. Only my brother-in-law knows for sure what's going on, and he's been sworn to silence. I doubt he's even told my sister."

"And you don't know anything about Dragon?"

I take a deep breath. "Only that I had to bail him out of jail last night for soliciting a prostitute."

Silence for a moment.

Then, "Uh...what?"

"You heard me, Ted. Didn't Antonio tell you?"

"I haven't heard from him—" She gasps. "Wait. That's right. Damn, I had a lot to drink. You left the party with Antonio."

"Yeah. We came back to my place, and we were... Well..."

"Don't you break my cousin's heart, Dee."

"Antonio and I didn't do anything. Dragon calling from the jail cell put an end to that. We didn't really have any chemistry anyway."

"That's a shame. It would be nice to have you for a cousin."

"Probably not happening, Ted, since I fucked another guy this morning. Anyway, we were sitting on the couch, talking, and that's when Dragon called to tell me he was at the station. Antonio went with me."

"That must've been a little awkward."

I can't help but laugh lightly. "You think?"

"So Dragon really tried to pick up a prostitute last night?"

"He says he didn't." I cup my hand over the phone and speak softly. "He says she propositioned *him*, and then said that she really needed the work because she hadn't eaten or something, so he just...*gave* her some money."

"Uh...okay." She scoffs. "Diana, have I told you about this great real estate opportunity I have for you? In a fucking swamp?"

"Ha. You're hilarious, Ted."

"Don't tell me you believe him."

I think for all of a few seconds before I say, "Yeah, Teddy. I *do* believe him."

She pauses before continuing. "You seem pretty sure."

"Well... I guess I am." I scratch my arm. "I mean, if I wasn't, I wouldn't have gone to bed with him this morning. I'm not about to play second fiddle to a hooker, for God's sake."

Teddy laughs into the phone. "That's for sure, Dee. You're usually pretty discriminating. When is the last time you got any, anyway?"

"About an hour ago," I deadpan.

"Ha! You know what I mean. Jason Majors was after you big time, and you didn't so much as bite."

She's right. Jason Majors is an architect at Teddy's firm, and he was my immediate supervisor for my internship. Really good-looking too, in a clean-cut way. But work is work, and I don't fraternize with coworkers.

"No, I didn't."

"I would have."

"Jason wasn't my type."

She chuckles. "Diana, Jason is *exactly* your type."

She's not wrong. And I was—am—attracted to Jason. But Dragon... It's so different, the way I want him. I can't explain it to Teddy. I can't even explain it to myself.

"He's not, really," I say. "Not that Dragon is either. And now things are weird. I feel like I have to walk on eggshells around here. Like he's going to think this can be a regular thing with us."

"I thought you said he explicitly said he wasn't offering a relationship."

"He did." I press my lips together. "But he might think I'm an easy lay for whenever he's in the mood. And I live all of a few feet from his bed."

"If you don't want to be his fuck buddy, you just have to tell him that's the case...unless you don't want it to be."

"No, of course not."

But the lie is bitter on my tongue.

Because already I'm thinking about the next time I can go

to bed with Dragon. How it will be even better now that we're beginning to learn each other's bodies and what we each like. Which, in my case, is anything he chooses to do to me.

"I bet he likes it rough," Teddy says.

I can't help a sly smile. "Not as rough as you might think. I mean, he told me it wouldn't be gentle, so I was expecting him to want to tie me to the bedposts or something."

"Rough doesn't necessarily mean bondage, Dee."

"I know that."

Except maybe I don't. Maybe I'm still naïve even at my age.

"There was something freeing about having him take charge," I say. "I didn't have to think about anything. I let him do what he wanted to do to me. I mean, I think he would've stopped if I told him to, but I didn't. I didn't have any desire to."

"Congratulations," she says.

"For what?"

"You have just released your innermost sexual prowess, Diana. Sex for the sake of sex. Who needs emotion anyway? All that does is lead to heartbreak. Why do you think Bud and Tracy have the understanding they've got going on? You get all the fun physical parts of a relationship and none of the dull emotionality."

I tug on my lip a minute, thinking about how to respond. I've never had my heart broken. I've never really cared enough about another human being that it was even an issue. I've dated. I've even been sort of serious on occasion. The relationships always ended, and it was usually a mutual decision. I was sad for a day or two, took the excuse to eat a pint of ice cream even though I knew I'd regret it, and then moved on without too much trouble.

Something tells me I wouldn't be able to move on that easily from Dragon...

"You still there?"

"Yeah, sorry. I was just thinking. What you said about emotion."

"Love stinks," Teddy says.

"I'm not sure I would know," I say.

She gasps. "You've never been in love? How have we never talked about this before?"

"Because we're usually talking about *your* exploits," I tell her. "I'm a good girl, remember?"

"Correction," she says with a chuckle. "You *were* a good girl. That train has officially left the station."

She's not wrong.

"Maybe. But I don't think it will leave the station again. For either of us."

"Hey, never say never, babe." She laughs. "Anyway, I've got to run. But call me tomorrow, okay? I want to hear about your first day."

"Absolutely. Will do." I end the call.

I've already taken my shower, and my damp hair is hanging around my shoulders. I'm sitting around in my bra and undies, so I pull on a pair of leggings and a large sweatshirt.

The time has come to face the music. I breathe in deeply and open my door.

Not that I expect to see Dragon. He's probably in his room. He was taking a shower when I sneaked out of his room following our tryst.

I pad out to the kitchen to get a drink of water, and I notice a few crumbs on the kitchen island counter.

He must've had a sandwich or something. Maybe that

means he's still here.

I should eat too, but I filled up on pizza last night. I'm not even that hungry yet.

"Dragon?" I say, not loudly.

No response, of course. If he's in his room, he wouldn't have heard me, and if he were anywhere else in the penthouse, I would've seen him.

I walk to his door and knock lightly.

And again, no response.

"Dragon?"

I turn his doorknob. It's open, which means he's probably not here.

I crack the door. "Dragon, are you home?"

No response, and the door to his bathroom is open and the light is off.

He's gone.

Well, what did I expect? He was ready to leave this morning. I merely waylaid him.

A wave of sadness settles over me as I gaze around the room. Then—

His backpack. His duffel bag.

They're still here.

I smile despite myself.

Dragon will be back.

I have no idea what to expect when he gets here, but he will be back.

And though I hate to admit it, I feel kind of giddy about that.

CHAPTER TWENTY-SIX

DRAGON

I like walking.

I always have. Helps me clear my head.

I need to find some work.

I don't have much cash on me, as I gave most of it to that hooker last night. The rest is in a checking account that I access from a debit card. I also have a credit card, but it's linked to my Snow Creek address, so that's where the bill would go.

Jesse was lecturing me all about how I should just download a mobile banking app and pay all my bills online, but I don't trust the tech companies with all that info. I mean, I'm sure they have it already, but they sure as hell are not going to get it from me. Plus, I feel like I'm a little more responsible with my money when I actually have to write a physical check every month to pay my bills.

I mostly deal in cash anyway. My last job—other than odd jobs and drumming for Dragonlock—was at a dispensary in Barrel Oaks.

Marijuana is legal in Colorado—has been for a while. But Donny Steel, Diana's older brother and the city attorney for our small western slope town of Snow Creek, has made it his goal in life to keep the dispensaries out. Well, it's not actually Donny. His mother, Jade Steel, was the city attorney for decades before she retired. I don't think Donny cares one way or another, but keeping Snow Creek pot-free means something to his mother, so he hasn't let any dispensaries in.

The city attorney of Barrel Oaks, however, had no qualms about selling weed. "Tax the hell out of it and funnel that money to our schools," she famously declared when the state first passed the constitutional amendment to legalize.

Working at a dispensary meant that I was paid in cash. Because marijuana is still federally illegal, most banks won't touch the businesses, so they operate on a solely cash basis. Sometimes I took my payment in some of their primo weed.

But those days are over. This time I've got to stay sober. And this time, I'm determined to stay away from all of it.

Other than that, I did odd jobs around town when people needed help. It was great because I was able to keep flexible hours. When you're part of a struggling band, you have to be ready to leave at a moment's notice to go play at some dive bar where you might catch a big break.

And that's exactly what happened. Dragonlock got its big break at a little bar in a small Utah town. Two members of Emerald Phoenix just happened to be in the audience and heard us play.

We each received ten grand as a signing bonus. The most money I've ever seen at one time. It was that way for all of us in the band.

Jesse and Rory may have married into the Steel fortune, but at the time we got that gig, the two of them really needed the money. A fire destroyed their family's vineyards, which was their livelihood. Most of their bonuses went to help out at home.

Most of mine went to pay for rehab, other than a couple

grand I socked away into my savings for emergencies. What I couldn't afford, Jesse and Brianna made up, and I'm determined to pay them back.

I'm determined to pay Diana back for all the rent as well for as long as I stay there.

But before I can do any of that, I've got to get some money coming in.

Not only do I need the cash, but I need something to do. What am I supposed to do while Diana is at work? Just lie around her penthouse and eat bonbons like a kept man?

The thought actually makes me smile a bit. Wouldn't be such a bad life. Being Diana Steel's boy toy.

But Diana Steel has no need or use for a boy toy. That kind of life would just make me hate myself anyway.

It took me a long time not to hate myself. Especially after my relapse. I've still got a long way to go, but I can at least tolerate myself these days. Barely, but it is what it is.

After an hour of walking, I'm on the edge of downtown. I've walked this way before, and I've spent time browsing the music store.

What the hell? I'll go in and see if they need any drumming instructors.

I've had private students before, back home on the western slope—students whose parents didn't think to ask what my education is.

Students whose parents have usually heard me play with Dragonlock and know I'm good.

But here in the store? They may want someone with a degree in music, like Jesse and Rory have.

I walk in anyway, instinctively heading straight for the displays of drum sets.

I have a pretty decent set of drums back home. I couldn't take my own set for our tour in Europe. We used rentals. Not that it mattered since I only played one concert.

Fuck. I don't want to go there right now. My therapist has told me time and again to leave the past in the past and focus on today.

If Jesse had kicked me out of the band, I wouldn't have had a lot of complaints. He had every right to. But he didn't. He was mad as a rabid dog for sure. But he got over it. He valued our friendship enough to give me another chance. Not to mention asking me to be his best man.

I swear to God, I will never let him down again.

Tim always says it has to be more about not letting *myself* down, not another person. Whatever.

My own self-worth was the least of Jesse's problems when I pulled that stunt in Europe. So why should *I* give a rat's ass about it now?

I sigh. I've got a long way to go.

Which is why this thing with Diana can't happen. How can I expect another person to accept me when I can barely tolerate myself?

I stroll through the drums, admiring them, and then head toward the sheet music section. I can spend hours here. Sheet music is like crack to me.

Damn, bad reference.

A new guitar and percussion piece stands out—or rather, its title does.

Griffin Sanctuary.

And of course I can't help myself. I pick it up and take a look.

Already, I can see it has a mythological vibe to it. It's

entirely instrumental, no vocals at all. Already I know that Dragonlock will never perform it, seeing as our main selling point is Jesse and Rory's combined vocals. But I look through the piece anyway, mesmerized by its intricacies.

The opening riff from the drum sets the scene, driving an intensely even rhythm section that propels the listener forward as if they're on the wings of the griffin. The drums then take center stage, commanding attention with earsplitting fills and funky grooves. Then the guitar riffs soar, weaving melodies over the pulsating rhythm section. Bass lines answer the guitar's question with a thunderous rumble.

Wow. What a beginning. It's like I'm reading the score to an epic film.

My heartbeat increases as I continue perusing the music. In the middle section, the instruments combine into a crescendo of raw energy and emotion, and then the drums unleash a barrage of rocking fills and driving rhythms, while the guitars wail and scream atonally.

But I almost drop the music to the floor when I reach the ending. Instead of finishing with a bang, the music slowly dies down until it fades into complete silence. As if the titular griffin has found its sanctuary—or maybe it's been slain by some stronger beast and has limped off into a tragic yet noble death.

Just like my own Griffin, I don't know what happens at the end. An invisible cord wraps around my heart.

God... Who wrote this? And why is it eerily reminiscent of the beast of burden inside me that I've tried to quell my entire life?

I turn back to the front page of the score. The composer's name is Dennis Friedrich. No one I've ever heard of. But

Dragonlock plays mostly original songs with the occasional cover. So even though I love looking at sheet music, I rarely buy any.

I certainly can't spend any money today—I don't have any—just because this piece of music stands out to me. I should put it down.

Forget about it.

But that would mean forgetting about Griffin, and though it pains me to remember, I can't allow myself to ever let her go.

I freaked out today when Diana touched the tattoo on my thigh. I don't think about it much. I just know it's there. I need to have Griffin with me. But I can't be able to see it, or I'll dwell on all those years lost.

And then I think about the young hooker last night—the one who got me thrown in the slammer. I'm usually pretty tight with my money. But something in her eyes reminded me of my little sister, and I couldn't help myself.

For a moment, my mind goes to the place I never wanted to go.

What if it *was* Griffin?

I shake the thought out of my head. No, that woman was way too young. Griffin would be twenty-seven by now. Older than Diana.

God...

That young girl... I'm not even sure she was eighteen.

Her skin was so light and rosy and beautiful, and her blue eyes—nearly as blue as Griffin's, even in the dim streetlights—should've been sparkling in her youth. Instead they were sunken and sad. Hard looking.

I wish I could've helped her.

But she no doubt took the money and gave it back to her

pimp.

Then he probably sent her out to find more.

And any more she got that night wouldn't have come as freely as mine did.

She'd have had to work for it.

I shake my head again to clear it of the unwanted images.

Griffin is gone. Most likely dead and buried.

All those years that I was away in the group homes, I thought maybe my parents would come and get me. Once Griffin disappeared, surely they'd realize they made a terrible mistake.

That I hadn't been the one to harm Griffin in the first place.

Someone had an eye on her, and for some reason, whoever it was got interrupted that first night.

As much as I would love to see her again, I know she's buried somewhere. Eternally five or six years old and at peace now.

Fuck it. I grab the sheet music and take it to the checkout counter.

"Is this all for you today?" a bright and cheery young woman says to me.

"Yeah. Thanks." Then I take a deep breath. "Are you looking for any percussion instructors at the moment?"

She frowns. "I have to check with the owner, and he's not in today. He takes Sundays off."

"Okay. Thanks anyway."

She grabs a pad of sticky notes from under the counter. "You want to leave your name and number? I'll be happy to give it to him tomorrow."

"Yeah, sure."

She hands me one of the sticky notes along with a pen. "Write your name and contact information on here. He'll be in tomorrow morning."

"Thanks." I scribble my name and number down on the back of the card and hand it to her, looking at her name tag. "I appreciate it, Annalise. That's a beautiful name."

"Thank you." She blushes. "Would you like a bag for your music?"

"Nope. I'll just carry it. I hope to hear from the owner tomorrow."

She bats her eyes. "I hope you hear from him, too. It would be nice to have you around here"—she looks down at the card—"Dragon." Her eyes widen.

I nod. "That's my name."

She leans forward. "I have to say you're the first Dragon I've ever met."

"And probably the last," I say. "Thanks for everything, Annalise."

Annalise gives me a wide smile. She's a cute little thing, can't be any more than nineteen or twenty, with a body of soft curves and a round and friendly face that's bordering on pretty.

I leave the music store, and... Now what? It's not quite dinnertime, although I can always eat.

But I just spent fifteen bucks I don't have on some sheet music I'll probably never use. Just because it bears my sister's name—the name I try not to think about but is always there.

Fuck it all.

I walk for another hour, breathing deeply, until I decide it's time to return. Walking past the rehab center, I'm tempted to go in. Former residents are allowed to pop in at any time and talk to one of the counselors on duty.

Sometimes we can even get a free meal out of it if we come at the right time.

It's too early for dinner, though.

I turn and head toward Diana's building. I suppose I have to talk to her eventually.

I just hope I can find the right words.

CHAPTER TWENTY-SEVEN

DIANA

I hate the designation of "business casual."

Growing up on a ranch, we never thought much about clothing. I probably thought more of it than my younger sister, Brianna. She was happy in jeans, a western shirt, and sparkling cowboy boots.

That's all we wore around the ranch when we were working. I may come from money, but we all were taught the value of a dollar and a hard day's work.

But I was the one who enjoyed fashion. Brianna couldn't care less about any of that. Once I got into high school, I'd go into the city on wild shopping sprees, looking for the latest and greatest dresses that I could wear at school dances.

Then, when I got to college and began to study architecture, I went for more of a professional look. I wear a lot of suits with either pants or pencil skirts complete with a blazer and basic pumps.

I assembled an entire closet full of beautiful business clothes, only to find out that my new firm—the biggest architecture firm in the state of Colorado—has now gone business casual with an even looser dress code on Fridays.

If I show up in one of my Diane von Furstenberg suits, I'll look like a complete outsider.

I spread several outfits out on my bed. Am I overthinking this?

Probably, but tomorrow will be my first day, and I need to make the right impression. Most of my suits would look way too zipped-up and unapproachable.

But a casual sweater and a pair of black slacks might not be enough.

"Ugh!" I shout out loud.

I don't like any of the clothes I've picked out.

I go back to my large walk-in closet and scan the racks once more.

What do you wear to the most sought-after job in any young architect's life—especially when you want to be assigned to their biggest project?

The office is business casual, and you don't want to look uptight.

My gaze finally falls on a pair of slacks. They're dark gray, and I hadn't considered them before because they're actually yoga pants made to look like slacks.

But man, they do accent my ass like nothing else. Those with a pair of black patent-leather pumps—or maybe I should go for regular pebbled leather—and a crisp white blouse might just be perfect.

But which white blouse? I decide on a fitted cotton number that is actually meant to be worn untucked. Because these pants are actually yoga pants, I can't wear a belt with them, so any other blouse wouldn't look right.

I heave a sigh of relief.

It's not perfect, but it will do. During my several interviews, I took note of what the other women were wearing. Very few of them wore dresses or skirts. I thought about going shopping and buying a whole new wardrobe for this job, but that seemed outrageous. Just because I can doesn't mean I should.

I'm happy with the outfit I chose, but then I start to panic again.

That's just for tomorrow. There are four more days in the week. Plus...casual Fridays.

Wearing jeans to work in a downtown architecture firm doesn't sit well with me. Sure, I grew up wearing jeans, but that was on a ranch.

I traipse through my walk-in closet, again pulling on various pieces of clothing and considering them. Is this how it will be now? Panicking until I know what I'm going to wear for every day of the week?

I finally hang everything back up. I'll worry about Tuesday's outfit tomorrow night.

If only I could just wear the same thing every day.

I walk out of my bedroom and into the kitchen to see what I can make myself for a quick supper.

The door opens, and I look over my shoulder to see Dragon walking in. He's carrying something. It looks like a paper of some sort.

My nipples harden, and I say a silent thank-you that I chose a padded bra today. I wish I knew what to say to him.

I settle on, "Hi."

"Hi," he says.

"I'm fixing some dinner. You want anything?"

"No, I'm fine." He glances toward the fridge and frowns. "I'll have a sandwich or something."

"I'm just making some pasta and sauce. It's no trouble."

He sits down at the counter, setting the paper he's carrying down in front of him. "Yeah, okay. If it's no trouble."

"What's that?" I gesture to the papers.

"Some sheet music. I stumbled upon this music store while I was out walking. Over on the edge of town."

"That must be Antonio's store."

"What?" he says.

"I told you this. The guy I met last night, he's the owner of a music store on the edge of town. It must be the same one you found."

"Oh, right. I left my name and number with the girl working the cash register," he says. "But I don't expect anything to come of it."

I grab my phone. "I can call Antonio. Or Teddy. They're cousins."

"No." He crosses his arms. "I don't want anyone getting a job for me. If they want to talk to me, they will."

"All right." I shake my head. "But I'm happy to help if you need it."

He looks down at the music. "You're already doing enough, letting me stay here."

I'm not sure how to respond to that, so I say nothing and turn back to the stove.

I feel Dragon's eyes on me as I heat up a jar of spaghetti sauce on the stove and boil water for the pasta.

I slice up some mushrooms for the sauce.

It'll be a veggie sauce tonight since I didn't get any ground beef out of the freezer. Guess I've been preoccupied about the new job.

Not to mention all the sex with the man I'm now cooking dinner for.

I look up. Dragon is getting up from the counter.

I hope he likes mushrooms. I should have asked before I

added them. I love a good mushroom sauce. It's as savory as meat with a lot fewer calories.

Plus, I ate more pizza than I should have last night. Luckily the excess cheese didn't bother me much, but unlike my sister, Brianna, I have to watch my weight. And yeah, that pisses me off.

Once everything's ready, I grab a couple of plates and place a hearty portion of pasta on one for Dragon, cover it with sauce, and add a few slices of Italian bread from the store. He's in the living area, looking at the music he bought.

"It's ready," I say. I set it on my small kitchen table.

Then I plate my own dinner, fill two glasses of water, and bring them all over to the table.

Dragon takes a seat in front of his plate. "Looks great."

Before I sit down, "I forgot napkins. Just a minute." I head back in the kitchen, grab the napkins out of their holder, and bring a few back to the table. I hand one to him. "Here you go."

He nods and places the napkin on his lap.

Then he twirls the spaghetti onto his fork like a champ.

I'm a little mesmerized by it.

I never mastered that. I cut my spaghetti and eat it with a fork.

"Where did you learn to do that?" I ask after he swallows. "Do what?"

"Twirl your spaghetti on a fork like that."

He thinks for a minute. "My mother. She's Italian." He frowns. "Or was Italian. I don't know if she's alive or not."

I nearly drop my jaw. Did he just open up to me about something?

He looks back down at his plate. Apparently he's done talking.

"So your parents..."

"I don't talk about my parents," he says to his plate.

"Oh, okay," I say. "Sorry."

Then I berate myself internally. What am I sorry for? He brought it up.

"I could never master it. My aunt Marjorie's a chef, and she does a mean Italian dinner. She's tried to show me time and time again since I was a little kid how to do it. But every time I tried, I either got a bunch of spaghetti strands hanging down, or the amount on my fork would be way too big to fit into my mouth."

Dragon doesn't respond. Just twirls more spaghetti on his fork and brings it to his lips.

God, those lips...

He does have gorgeous lips.

"I'm glad you like mushrooms," I say.

"Yeah." He twirls another forkful of spaghetti.

Now I'm curious. Curious about his Italian mother. Curious about his parents. About his childhood. About all those things that he never talks about.

About that tattoo on the back of his thigh.

About why he gave money to a freaking hooker.

I get feeling sorry for the woman. But he had to know exactly where that money would end up. It wasn't going to help her. It was going to help her pimp.

But Dragon is not going to answer any of my questions.

He's simply going to live in my house, eat my food, apparently, and keep to himself.

Unless we're fucking like bunnies.

Though I doubt that will happen again.

I'd like to tell him that it meant something to me. That he

fulfilled a need, and I'm grateful.

I can't bring myself to talk to him at all.

So I finish my spaghetti, sop up the excess sauce with my slice of bread, wipe my lips with my napkin, drain my glass of water, and take my plate to the sink.

Dragon is finishing up as well.

"There's more if you'd like another helping," I say.

"Yeah, if you don't mind."

"Not at all."

I walk to the table, take his plate, serve him what's left over, about half a helping, and hand it back to him along with another slice of bread.

He doesn't say thank you, but I don't expect it.

I don't think he means to seem ungrateful. I just don't think he knows how to act. He's always been quiet and dark. And he's probably embarrassed by what happened between us.

He doesn't need to be embarrassed about that. I enjoyed every minute of it. In fact, I've had a hard time not thinking about it.

Worrying about my wardrobe didn't get it out of my mind. I tried to sit down and read, which also didn't help.

Nothing's going to get my mind off him.

Nothing until I start that job tomorrow.

Then I'll have so much to think about, I won't be able to give Dragon Locke a second thought.

At least I hope not.

I wipe my mouth with my napkin again. "Put your dishes in the sink when you're done. Or better yet, rinse them off and shove them into the dishwasher. I only run a load when it's full."

He nods, grunting.

I leave the kitchen, head back to my bedroom, and turn on

the television.

As usual, with nearly six hundred channels, I can't find anything to watch.

I don't know why I pay for cable anymore. Most of my friends only get streaming services. Mental note—call the cable company first thing tomorrow and cancel everything.

My phone rings with a number I'm not familiar with.

Normally, I ignore numbers I don't know, but after yesterday and Dragon's call, I can't. What if it's another emergency? Someone who needs me?

"Hello," I say into the phone.

"Hi, Diana. It's Antonio Carbone."

I nearly drop the phone. I certainly didn't think that I'd be hearing from him again, not after last night.

"Hi, how are you?"

"Good, good. I dropped by my store for a minute this evening to check on a few things, and my cashier told me your friend Dragon had been in looking for a drumming instructor job."

"He told me he stopped by a music store. I figured it might be yours."

"My cashier was pretty smitten. She wants me to hire him. But given the fact that you had to bail him out of jail last night..."

"Right. You want my opinion on the matter."

"Let's just say I'm going to need a reference. What can you tell me about him?"

Despite the fact that he gave me the best sex I've ever had, I barely know him. Still, I want him to get the position, so I tell Antonio what I do know.

"He's my sister's husband's best friend. You know about

their band, Dragonlock. You know how they opened for Emerald Phoenix."

I leave out the tidbit that Dragon wasn't part of that tour—at least not after the first night.

"And he's your roommate. And he was arrested last night."

"Yeah. I suppose you're right."

"I'd like to give the guy a break," Antonio says. "But I'm a little apprehensive given the fact that he was caught soliciting."

"He claims he wasn't. He said he was just giving the woman some money out of the goodness of his heart. She gave him some sob story about getting in trouble with her pimp, so he gave her the money he had on him. And then of course the cops thought... I guess I don't have to spell it out."

"You believe him?"

I don't even have to think about my response. "Absolutely, I believe him. He's been through a rough time, and he's trying to get back on his feet."

"Rough time?"

Uh-oh. I said too much. I can't tell Antonio that Dragon is an addict. That would really be breaching a confidence. Dragon never said it was a secret, but it's not my place to tell anyone about it. Certainly not a potential employer.

"Yeah. I don't know all the details. And I didn't ask. I don't consider any of it my business."

"Diana, the guy lives with you. Don't you have a right to know a little bit about him?"

I know more about Dragon Locke. Biblically, at least. But the man who was trying to make out with me last night probably doesn't need to know that.

"I know all I need to know about him," I say. "He's a truly gifted percussionist, and I trust the opinions of my brother-in-law and sister. They adore him."

Antonio sighs into the phone. "Well, it'll make Annalise happy. She was a giggling schoolgirl over him when I stopped in the store earlier tonight."

Annalise? I don't ask. She must be the cashier Antonio mentioned.

"I don't think you'll be sorry. He truly is gifted. My brother-in-law says he's the best at drums he's ever seen. I mean, if Emerald Phoenix was impressed, wouldn't everyone else be?"

Antonio chuckles through the phone. "You got me there, Diana. Right. I'll give him a call first thing tomorrow and tell him he's got the job if he wants it."

My heart leaps. Why I'm so excited for Dragon is beyond me, but I am. I want what's best for him.

"And while you're on the phone," Antonio continues, "would you like to have dinner with me Friday night?"

And there it is. A lump in my throat. Because Antonio is a nice guy, and I like him. But damn... Dragon and I...

Except Dragon and I are absolutely nothing.

He made no promises. Made it clear he could make no promises.

Antonio is Teddy's cousin, and he owns his own business. I didn't think we had much chemistry at first, but maybe I'm wrong. "You know? I'd like that, Antonio."

"Great. I can probably find your place again, but give me your address anyway. I'll pick you up there around seven on Friday."

"Perfect." I rattle off my address. "See you then."

"I look forward to it."

I end the call.

Good. I have a date with a nice guy. A handsome guy. A guy who owns his own business, makes a decent living, doesn't seem to have any baggage.

I should be thrilled.

So why am I longing for a drummer with baggage the size of Texas?

CHAPTER TWENTY-EIGHT

DRAGON

I sit for a few minutes at the table after Diana leaves.

I stare down at the smudges of spaghetti sauce on my plate, at my empty glass of water.

My phone sits next to me. I don't labor under any delusion that I'll get a drumming job from that music store I walked into.

Especially not tonight. Especially not from the guy who escorted Diana to bail me out of freaking jail.

No one else really calls me, other than Jesse, and he's on his honeymoon.

So I'm surprised as hell when it rings.

I don't recognize the number, but I pick it up anyway. "Yeah?" I say into the phone.

"I'm looking for Dragon Locke," a low voice says.

"You found him. Who is this?"

"I know where your sister is."

The call ends.

My heart nearly stops as it drops to my stomach.

The spaghetti I just ate threatens to erupt from my mouth. What the fuck?

I quickly hit the number to call it back.

It rings, rings, rings...

But no one answers. Not that I expect anyone to.

How do you trace a call? How do you find where a number originated?

I don't have a fucking clue, but Diana might.

Griffin is screaming.

I'm only nine years old, but I'm so close to my little sister, and our rooms are right next to each other. Mom and Dad's room is on the other side of the small house.

So I get there first.

I get there first.

"It hurts, Dragon. It hurts!"

Blood.

Blood on her sheets, on her body, her pajamas—her pink flannel pajamas with blue hearts on them. Blood dripping from a cut on her round little cheek.

I can't speak. I only look.

Something...

Someone hurt Griffin.

Her window is open. That's how they must've gotten into her room.

There's a cut on her face, right down her cheek.

Another one on her shoulder.

Another one on her belly.

I freeze for a moment. Unsure what to do.

Tears are streaming down my sweet baby sister's face. "Help me, Dragon! Help me!"

On her nightstand, next to her bed, is a bloody knife.

I pick it up. Look at it.

That's when my parents walk in.

Griffin went into shock after that. She wouldn't talk. Couldn't talk. Went numb, her eyes glazed over.

I screamed and cried and told my parents I hadn't done it.

But you were holding the knife, they said.

A knife that came from our own kitchen, they said.

Did it? I didn't know.

The beginning of the end.

Because whoever hurt Griffin that night came back several months later.

And this time they took her away.

I didn't know that, of course. Not until years after the fact.

Did my parents truly think I had escaped the group home they had forced me into and come back and taken my little sister?

They must've thought so, because they didn't come to get me.

They never reclaimed me.

Griffin disappeared.

This isn't something I talk about. No one knows about Griffin except Jesse and Tim. So who could be calling? I trust both Jesse and Tim, so how would anyone else know? And why would he be messing with me?

But...

What if it's true? If this person knows where Griffin is, does that mean they know where her body is? Her tiny five-year-old body, decomposed by now?

Or...

Is Griffin alive?

No.

She can't be.

They wouldn't come to me. They'd go to my parents.

But I have no idea if my parents are even alive. I gave up caring about them decades ago.

They forsook me, so I forsook them.

But I have to know.

I have to know if this phone message was real or if it was just a horrible trick.

I walk to Diana's room and knock.

She opens the door just as she's ending a call. "Dragon?"

I swallow. "I don't want to bother you, but I need your help."

"With what?"

"Do you know how to trace a call?"

She shakes her head. "No, but my family has resources. What's going on?"

I pull up the number on my phone. "I just got a call from this number. I need to find out who it belongs to. Where it came from."

She takes a look at it. "It's a Denver area code, so it couldn't have come from far. Unless of course it's someone with a cell phone with a Colorado number who is now living somewhere else."

"Fuck." I rub my forehead. "You're right. It could've come from anywhere."

"I can call my dad. He has investigators he uses. Maybe they could figure it out."

I shake my head. "I'm sure I can't afford that."

She holds up a hand. "My dad has them on retainer. They probably wouldn't mind doing it as a favor."

"I'm not in any situation to ask anyone in your family for

another favor," I say. "I'm already living here."

She frowns. "Dragon, what is this about? What did that person say to you?"

I close my eyes for a moment. When I look at Diana—at her beautiful caring eyes—I almost want to tell her everything. I could so easily vomit out the entire story. More than I've even told my therapist. More than I even told Jesse.

But can I trust Diana Steel?

Better yet—do I *want* to trust Diana Steel?

Because I don't trust anyone. Besides Jesse. I'm not even sure I trust my therapist, though he hasn't done me wrong yet.

"I just need to know where the call came from. If it's legit or not."

"Dragon, you don't have to tell me if you don't want to." She places a hand on my shoulder. "But if I call my father and have him get in touch with our investigators, you will have to tell *them*."

I ignore the jolt of electricity coursing through my body at her touch. "Why would they need to know what was said? Can't they just figure out where the call came from?"

"It's not that simple. They need all the information to do a thorough investigation. Whatever they said to you might be some clue as to where they are, what they want, why this even happened."

"They didn't say they wanted anything."

"Fine." She looks me dead in the eyes. "But if I call them, if I get our investigators to help you, you have to tell them everything. You get it?"

I heave in a deep breath. "Fine. I wouldn't even ask except..."

"Except what?"

"Except...nothing."

"This is important to you," she says.

"You think?"

She frowns.

I run my hands through my hair, sighing. "I'm not trying to be rude, Diana. This... This..." No more words come.

She removes her hand from my shoulder and cups my cheek. Her touch is soothing. More soothing than it should be.

"Something is inside you," she says. "I don't think you're as dark and sinister as you claim to be."

I shake my head. "You don't know me."

"You're right. I don't. I know next to nothing about you." She looks into my eyes, narrowing her own. "But I can see that this is important to you. I see it in those eyes of yours. I see emotion in their depths. Emotion I wasn't sure you had until..."

"Until what? Tonight?"

She bites her lip. "Until this morning."

This morning? Is she serious? What happened between us had no emotion whatsoever. I open my mouth to say so, but no words come out.

She drops her hand from my face and then reaches into her pocket to grab her cell phone. "I'll call my father. He'll know what to do."

All I can do is nod and leave Diana's room so she can make the call in private. I saunter over to her living room and plant myself on her couch.

A few moments later she comes back out.

"An investigator is coming over," she says. "He's going to need to look at your phone. I'll leave the room if you want me to, but you're going to need to tell him everything."

I nod. "Thank you."

A smile spreads over her face.

"What?" I demand.

She slaps her hand over her mouth. "The smile isn't because I'm happy you're going through something difficult. I'm not, Dragon. I can see that you're hurting, and I don't like that one bit. But you said thank you."

With a slow exhale, tension draining from my shoulders, I meet her gaze. "Yeah, I have a hard time with that."

She crosses the living room and lowers herself onto the love seat. "I know you do. Why?"

I take a deep breath. "I'm not used to people being nice to me. I'm not used to people doing something for me out of the goodness of their hearts. It's usually because they want something in return."

Her eyes soften. "Why do you think that?"

I can't answer that question because someone raised the way Diana was raised will never understand. She was raised with everything she could ever want, with two loving parents who would never think of sending her away.

She was raised with enough money to have everything she desired. Enough food. A life without bullies, without evil, without horror.

"You going to answer me?" she asks.

"I can't. It's beyond your comprehension."

Her hands whip to her hips. "Excuse me?"

"I don't mean that in a bad way. I just mean there's no way you can ever understand why I have a problem with gratitude." I place my hand over my heart. "It's not that I don't feel it."

She frowns. "You just can't say it."

I drop my hand to my side. "Seems that every time I said it in the past, it came back to bite me in the ass. Bite me *hard* in the ass."

"I'll never bite you in the ass." Her eyes brighten. "Unless you ask me to."

My cock responds to those words.

And that's the last thing I need.

This—whatever it is—between Diana and me has to go on the back burner. It needs to be taken off the stove altogether. The phone call... Griffin... I need to find out what it all means.

Damn, I could sure use a fucking drink.

All these years, I assumed Griffin was dead.

She probably is. This could just be some cruel prank.

But no one knows. No one but my parents. My therapist. And Jesse.

"I shouldn't have said that," she says.

I cross my arms. "Diana, I am no good for you, and we both know it."

She gets up off the love seat and sits next to me on the couch, thumbing the stubble on my cheek. "Maybe. Maybe not." She sighs. "I start that new job tomorrow, and I won't have time for any of this anyway. So once we talk to the investigator tonight, you're on your own."

"No different from any other time in my life," I say.

She checks the time on her phone. "He'll be here in about ten minutes."

I open my eyebrows. "That quickly?"

She nods. "My family pays this company a lot of money. They're on call twenty-four seven."

Damn. Is there nothing that money can't buy?

Happiness, I suppose.

Diana's happy, though. All the Steels seem to be.

Who wouldn't be with riches beyond anyone's wildest

dreams?

But then I think about that bomb Diana dropped on me about her brothers and her father. They were victims of human trafficking. She didn't give me any details beyond that, but I can't imagine it was anything good.

Money can get you a lot of things, but I'm not sure it can fix something like that.

And I'm not sure it can fix my current problem, either.

"You want me to sit with you while you talk to them?"

"No."

I don't mean to be so forceful, but if she sits with me, she'll learn the truth. That my own parents believed the worst of me.

That I learned to believe the worst of myself.

I'll have to make sure this guy who comes over here will hold what I say in confidence, even from the people who pay his bills.

I open my mouth to say as much when someone buzzes the intercom.

Diana walks toward the door. "That'll be him. Let's go." She presses the intercom button. "Yes?"

"Hi. It's Alayna Johansson from Infinite Security. Mr. Talon Steel sent me over."

"Yeah, thank you. I'm his daughter Diana. Come on up."

"Not a him after all," I say.

"I guess it's a her." Diana's cheeks flush pink.

A few moments later, a knock on the door. Diana opens it.

Alayna Johansson is gorgeous. Blond and blue-eyed and totally stacked.

Doesn't even get my blood moving.

"Diana?" She holds out her hand. "I'm Alayna Johansson."

Diana shakes her hand. "So nice to meet you, and thank

you for coming over so quickly. Come on in."

She steps inside.

"This is Dragon Locke," Diana says. "He's the one who will be talking to you."

"Great." She extends her hand again. "Nice to meet you, Dragon."

I take Alayna's outstretched hand. It's warm. Inviting. Still doesn't do a thing for me.

Alayna scans the room. "Where should we speak?"

Diana smiles. "I think Dragon wants to talk to you in private. I can go to my bedroom. Feel free to use the kitchen table. Or the living area if you'd like."

Alayna nods. "Okay. Thank you, Diana."

Diana disappears into her bedroom.

Alayna gestures to the small kitchen table. "Sometimes it's easier to talk when you're sitting."

I take a seat across from her.

Alayna sets her phone on the table. "Mr. Steel didn't tell me much, other than that you received a phone call that distressed you a bit. And you want to know where and who it came from."

I nod slowly. "That's about the gist of it."

"May I take a look at your phone?"

"Yeah." I unlock it and hand it to her.

She taps on the screen, looking up my recent calls. "So this is the number." She pulls an iPad out, sets it up, starts typing on it. "Looks like you called the number a few seconds after the call ended. I'm assuming it just rang and didn't go to voicemail?"

"That's correct."

"All right. Let me take a look here." She types several

things into her iPad. "Nothing's coming up right away, which is per usual, but we have to try all the standard avenues first. Can you tell me exactly what the person on the other line said?"

"It was a low voice. A man. And he said my name. And then he said, 'I know where your sister is.'"

She looks up. "Is your sister missing?"

I lower my voice. "This is confidential, correct?"

"Of course."

And I begin.

CHAPTER TWENTY-NINE

DIANA

As I step through the polished glass doors of the building that houses Lund & Lopez, my heart races with a mixture of excitement and nerves. This is the moment I've been waiting for—my first day as a professional architect at one of the top firms in Colorado. The lobby is adorned with architectural models, photos of ornate buildings, and plush seating. I take a deep breath, steeling myself for the day ahead.

Dragon and his meeting with the investigator try to edge their way into my mind, but I don't let them. He didn't talk to me last night after Alayna left, and I left this morning before he came out of his room.

I take the elevator to the top floor. A receptionist greets me with a warm smile as I approach the front desk. "Good morning, and welcome to Lund & Lopez. How can I help you?"

"I'm Diana Steel. I start work today."

"Right, of course." She pulls something up on her computer screen. "Mr. Reynolds told me you'd be here this morning."

I return her smile. "I'm excited to be here."

"Great to have you," she says. "Mr. Reynolds is in his office. It's down the hallway to your right, next to Mr. Lund's office on the corner. His door should be open."

I nod. "I should go right in?"

"Yeah. He said to send you to him when you got here."

I give her a nod of thanks, and once I leave the reception area, I enter a hive of activity, with architects and designers engaged in animated conversations and poring over blueprints at sleek, minimalist workstations.

No one gives me a second glance as I walk to the office. The gold nameplate says *Rodrigo Reynolds*. The door stands ajar, inviting me in. Still, I knock softly.

Mr. Reynolds, presumably, looks up from his desk. "Yes?"

I wave timidly. "Hi. I'm Diana Steel."

He flashes me a big corporate smile. "Diana, welcome." He rises. "Please come in."

"Thank you, Mr. Reynolds." I take a few steps into his office.

"Call me Rod. Have a seat." He gestures to a leather chair on the other side of his desk.

Rod is tall with dark hair, though it's graying around his temples. He's wearing khakis and a white button-down, no tie. I guess this is what he considers business casual. His office is spacious, with floor-to-ceiling windows offering panoramic views of Denver. The walls are adorned with architectural sketches and framed awards. Mr. Reynolds—Rod—is clearly a respected expert.

"Let's get started." Rod pulls out a folder from his desk. "Here's a project we're currently working on—a mixed-use development downtown. We're in the initial stages of design, and I'd like you to take a look and offer your insights."

I accept the folder, slightly disappointed that it's not the mountaintop project. But this is my first day. You don't send a rookie into the majors. I flip through the plans and sketches, envisioning the possibilities for the project. This particular development is a great candidate for vertical urban farming. Portions of the building's facade or rooftop could be dedicated to hydroponic or aeroponic agriculture, providing fresh produce to residents and local businesses and promoting self-efficiency. There are also spaces that could be used as pop-up shops, coworking areas, or event venues. One particular area could serve as an interactive art installation. I could get my cousin Gina—the artist of the family—to come down and help me out with that.

I expect Rod to ask me what I think, but instead he takes the folder from me. "Look at me, handing you work as soon as you arrive. We should take a tour of the office first. Who did you do your interview with?"

I try to hide my disappointment that he didn't ask me for my thoughts. "Um... It was someone in HR named Kathleen, and then I spoke to Mr. Lopez and to Ms. Wallace."

He nods. "Good, good. Judith Wallace is no longer with the firm, and Mr. Lopez is on vacation for the next two weeks. I'm handling his projects while he's gone. He's requested that you work with me, and if we work well together, he'll probably pair us up permanently."

I paste a smile on my face. "Sounds good."

Rod introduces me to my new colleagues and gives me a glimpse into the collaborative and dynamic culture of the firm. We pass through open-plan workspaces filled with drafting tables and computer stations. He shows me the break room, which has several vending machines and—I wasn't expecting this—an air hockey table. There's also a small kitchen with a full-sized stainless-steel fridge for employees to store their lunches, and an outdoor patio area where employees are encouraged to bring their work on sunny days.

After introducing me to myriad coworkers, most of whose names I promptly forget, Rod shows me to my work area and leaves me alone with the file he gave me in his office.

"Take a look and think about your ideas. We'll go to lunch to discuss them."

"Lunch?"

"Yes." He raises an eyebrow. "You do eat lunch, don't you?"

I eye his left hand. He's wearing a wedding band. This is just a lunch. I'm not sure why I'm reading something into it that's not there.

"Of course. What time?"

"I assume you have lunch around the same time as every other human being." He chuckles, then checks his watch. "I'll stop by your workstation around twelve thirty. I'm interested to hear what you have to say about this project."

"I look forward to it. Thanks for the tour."

"Anytime." He smiles. "See you in a few hours."

I delve back into the file and begin making notes.

The time passes quickly, and when Rod collects me, I take my iPad and follow him out of the office and into the elevator. We end up at a café on the first floor of the building.

"So what do you think of the project, Diana?" he asks once we're seated in a corner booth.

I grab my iPad. "I like it a lot," I say. "I wrote down my thoughts and—"

He takes the iPad out of my hands. "Let me see. I like to see what you write down even more than what you say. It helps me understand your process."

I blink. "Uh...sure. Of course."

Not what I was expecting, but I'm glad I took the time to reread my notes before lunch. Otherwise they might not make a lot of sense. My typing is terrible and usually fraught with errors.

Rod peruses them intently, pausing only to order a drink and then lunch when our server comes by.

My nerves are skittering. I honestly can't tell what he might be thinking. His expression is completely noncommittal.

My salad arrives, and he gestures for me to go ahead and eat.

I'm halfway done when he finally looks up.

I find myself holding my breath. Until, finally—

He slowly nods. "Nice work, Diana."

I swallow the bite I've been chewing. "Thank you."

I expect him to elaborate, but instead, "When we get back to the office, I want you to familiarize yourself with our current portfolio. See what jumps out at you."

I cock my head. "You're not assigning me to anything?"

He smiles. "Not just yet. You'll find a series of reports on your desk when we get back. Take a look, and then we'll talk again first thing in the morning."

"All right. Thank you."

I don't have to worry about small talk during the rest of lunch, as Rod enthralls me—or rather, seems to enthrall himself—with tales of his successes in the field.

I'm glad to be back in my office where I find the reports, meticulously organized by Rod's assistant. They contain a wealth of information about each project's scope, timeline, budget, and key milestones. I pore over them and absorb every detail.

One report in particular catches my eye—a comprehensive

analysis of a residential development project in the heart of the city that aims to revitalize a historic neighborhood with a mix of modern condominiums, townhouses, and green spaces, all while preserving the area's nineteenth-century charm and atmosphere.

The project sounds challenging, and I find myself thinking seriously about asking to be involved with it, but then I get to the next report.

The mountaintop resort—the reason I took this position.

My curiosity guides me, and I delve into the plans, poring over blueprints and sketches in search of inspiration and insight. The resort's design is breathtaking—a seamless blend of rustic charm and modern luxury, with sweeping views of snow-capped peaks and lush pine forests stretching as far as the eye can see.

But as I study the plans more closely, a nagging sense of unease gnaws at the edges of my consciousness. There's something missing—something crucial that I can't quite put my finger on.

I trace my finger along the lines of the blueprint. What am I missing?

It's not until I zoom in on the water supply system that I notice the flaw—a crucial pipeline that runs perilously close to the edge of a steep cliff, vulnerable to erosion and potential landslides.

This can't be possible, can it? These are the best architects and designers in Denver. In Colorado. Some of the best in the whole country. Surely they're aware of this. Perhaps I'm overthinking. They must have considered all possibilities and decided this was the best way to go. I mean, it's unlikely that anything could happen.

But damn...

The top of a mountain is not the place to take shortcuts.

But what if...?

A single failure in the pipeline could disrupt the entire water supply to the resort, jeopardizing the safety and comfort of its visitors.

Are these plans final? I shuffle through everything. Nothing notes that they're final, but they don't say draft either.

With a sense of urgency, I sketch out alternative routes for the pipeline, mapping out a path that avoids the unstable terrain and minimizes the risk of catastrophic failure. It's a challenging task, requiring careful consideration of topography, geology, and environmental impact, but I'm determined to find a solution that ensures the long-term sustainability and safety of the resort.

The problem?

It will cost more money.

A *lot* more money.

I gather my notes, rise, and walk to Rod's office, knocking on the door. When there's no answer, I open the door. His lights are out. I look across to his assistant's desk. She's gone as well.

What time is it, anyway?

I look down at my watch. Seven p.m. I've put in a full day, but I hate leaving without talking to Rod about my findings.

A few offices are still occupied, but I don't know any of my colleagues well enough yet to bring this to their attention.

I sigh.

I'll go home. Run a hot bath.

And deal with this tomorrow.

CHAPTER THIRTY

DRAGON

I don't hear from Alayna all day, and Diana doesn't come home in the evening. Worry grabs the back of my neck.

But why worry? It's a new job, and she already told me she'd be working late and would hardly be home.

I make myself a sandwich and decide to settle in for the night. Not like I have anything better to do anyway.

Until my phone rings. I don't know the number, and my heart starts to hammer. Maybe it's the person who called about Griffin.

"Yeah?" I say into the phone.

"Is this Dragon Locke?" It's a different voice from before.

"It is."

"Hey, Dragon, I don't know if you remember me, but we met... Never mind."

My heart is still pounding. I will it to slow.

"I'm sorry, who are you?"

"I'm Antonio Carbone."

"Ah..." I take a deep breath. "We met the night I...got arrested."

"We did." He laughs—sort of. "Sorry. Didn't want to bring that up."

"Not a problem. What can I help you with?"

"I don't know if Diana mentioned it to you, but I run the music store on the edge of town. I'm the owner."

"Oh."

"You made quite an impression on my cashier, and we do need percussion instructors. I was wondering when you could start."

"Now?"

He chuckles into the phone. "I have about ten students on a waiting list for percussion instruction. The pay is forty dollars an hour."

"Yeah? And what's your cut?"

"My cut is fifty percent. But you get forty an hour. I collect eighty from the student and pay you half."

"Is this on a contract basis or an employment basis?"

"Contract. It won't include any benefits, and no taxes will be withheld from your income."

Damn. I can't live on forty bucks an hour if it's only part-time.

"Fifty percent is a pretty steep cut," I say.

"It's what I charge, Dragon. You're using my instruments and my studios. You're certainly welcome to try to get students on your own if you'd rather."

He makes a good point. Man, I don't like this guy. But I need the income. Something is better than nothing. And word travels fast among parents looking for music lessons for their kids. Maybe I can find some extra students that I can teach privately for full price.

"Good enough. I'll take it. Let me know when I can start."

"I'll get in touch with the people on my waiting list, and I'll give you a call tomorrow. I imagine some of them will want to get started right away."

"So I'll have ten students. Is that weekly?"

"Yeah, and they have to sign up for ten lessons at once, so that'll give you four hundred dollars a week for at least ten weeks."

Who the hell can live on that? At least Diana's not making me pay rent, and so far she hasn't kicked me out.

"Great. I'll look forward to your call," I say.

"Glad to have you on board, Dragon."

The call ends, and I think about those words.

Glad to have you on board.

He just hired a man who, for all he knows, solicited a prostitute two nights ago.

He also didn't ask about my education. Would he be surprised to know I don't have a degree in music?

There's only one reason for any of this.

He wants to get into Diana's pants.

Fuck.

I wish that didn't bother me as much as it does.

I'm still holding my phone when it rings again.

Another number I don't recognize...

My heartbeat starts to accelerate once again.

"Yeah?"

"Call off your dog."

An icy chill runs up and down my spine when I realize it's the same voice from last night.

"Excuse me?"

"You want to find your sister? Call off your dog."

"What the fuck are you talking about?"

"The PI. Call her off."

"Then tell me. Tell me where my sister is."

"I can't guarantee your safety or hers while you've got

people sniffing around. Call. Her. Off."

The line goes dead.

Damn it.

Seriously?

Alayna told me I could call her anytime, and I'm ready to punch in her number when—

Call off your dog.

I don't for a minute think this person knows where Griffin is. I'm still convinced she's dead.

But what if...

What if he's telling the truth?

What if she *is* alive, and she's in danger, and the fact I'm talking to an investigator is exacerbating that danger?

Is that a chance I can take?

I'm glad Diana's not home. Not that I could tell her anything about this, but she was kind enough to bring in an investigator to help me.

How am I supposed to tell her that I have to call it off?

Fuck.

Fuck, fuck, fuck.

I call the number back.

Not that I expect anyone to answer.

Was it even the same voice? It sounded like it was. But it's not like I have recordings to compare the two.

There's no way of knowing anything.

This is so fucked up.

I got a new job—that won't pay me a living wage—from a guy who just wants to get into my roommate's pants. The same roommate I fucked into oblivion twenty-four hours ago.

I'm getting weird phone calls about my sister who I assumed has been dead for over twenty years. I got a PI by the grace of Diana, and now I'm told I have to call her off or whoever the fuck this is can't guarantee Griffin's safety. Assuming she actually is alive.

Oh, and of course, I'm out on bail for soliciting a prostitute.

Not to mention that my sobriety is hanging on by a fucking thread.

The only thing stopping me from running to the nearest liquor store and downing an entire case of beer is the memory of what my last relapse did to my best friend in the world and his band—*my* band.

But damn, I could sure use a hit right now. Fuck, it doesn't even need to be a hit. Just a beer. Something to take the edge off.

Thank God Diana doesn't keep anything in the house, or I'd be swallowing it down.

One thing's for sure.

If there's a chance that Griffin is alive...I can't screw this up.

Do I call off Alayna?

Maybe try to deal with this myself?

If I do that, I'll have to talk to the two people I swore I would never look in the face again.

My parents.

I don't even know where the hell they are. Or if they're even alive.

I remember their address in a northern suburb of Denver called Thornton.

The house was all red brick, a small ranch. Olive-green carpeting, which actually wasn't a bad thing because nothing would stain it.

I remember how Griffin would spit up on it all the time

when she was a baby, and my mother just brought over a rag, wiped up the puke, and you couldn't even tell.

I still remember the phone number too. The landline. Hell, they may not even use that anymore.

They probably don't live in that house.

But there is one way to find out.

It's seven o'clock. At least I know I have some money coming in soon, so I call a rideshare service and put in my parents' address.

CHAPTER THIRTY-ONE

DIANA

What a first day.

I'm exhausted. I'm excited and thrilled to read more about the mountaintop project.

But not thrilled that I found a pipeline issue that could be a potential liability.

I can't think about that right now. I place the blueprints on the kitchen counter.

I'm starving but too exhausted to make anything and too hungry to wait around for food to be delivered. I grab a protein shake out of the refrigerator, pop it open, pour a tall glass of ice water, and head straight to my bedroom.

And it's not until I'm in my bathroom running a hot bath with lavender essential oil that I consciously realize that Dragon's not home.

Nope.

It's not my place to worry. Or even to care.

So he's out. Doing...something. I don't care.

Except that's a big fat lie.

I *do* care.

Somehow, he has edged himself into my heart. And not just because of the great fuck we shared.

Because that's all it was—a great fuck. To think he was

feeling anything more than that would be ridiculous on my part. He went out of his way to tell me that it was a onetime thing.

But take sex out of the equation, and he's still occupying my thoughts. I actually care about the guy.

I sigh, strip my clothes off, and throw them in my hamper. I step into the warm, inviting tub.

I sink my entire body into the water, turn on the jets, close my eyes, and try to relax.

My sister-in-law Ashley, who's married to my older brother Dale, taught me this relaxation technique once. She has something called synesthesia, where she sees colors for sounds and sounds for colors and a bunch of other stuff that I don't understand, so this probably works a lot better for her.

I begin by breathing deeply in and visualizing the dark red of my root chakra at the base of my spine that represents foundation and grounding, our connection to the earth. Once I feel secure in the dark red, I change the color in my mind to my sacral chakra, which is represented by the color orange and is located in my lower abdomen, below my belly button. According to Ashley, this is a very important chakra for me because it represents creativity.

Once I see the red and the orange vividly, I move upward to my solar plexus chakra, which is yellow. This is in the upper abdomen, below the rib cage, and is linked to self-confidence and self-esteem.

Red, orange, yellow.

I repeat the colors in my mind, visualize each of them moving up my body.

I move on to the heart chakra, which is green. Ashley says this one is pink for her because green isn't the color of the heart. I prefer to use green so the colors go in the order of the rainbow. Makes more sense to me.

Red, orange, yellow, green.

Red, orange, yellow, green.

Onward to the throat chakra, which is blue and linked to communication and authenticity.

This is where I need help. How am I going to communicate to Rod that his team made a huge mistake on that project? And how am I going to communicate about...well, anything with Dragon?

No.

Not thinking about that now.

Red, orange, yellow, green, blue.

Breathe in, breathe out.

Breathe in...red, orange, yellow, green, blue...

Then the third eye, and this is where it gets slightly weird for me because sometimes I actually think I'm seeing something from that third eye, even though my eyes are closed. The third eye is indigo, that deep blue that hovers between blue and purple.

Here lies my intuition, and I'm going to need that tomorrow.

Hell, I need that with Dragon as well.

I breathe in, visualize all the colors from red to indigo flowing up my body, through all my chakras, until I get to the final one.

The crown chakra in the top of my head. It's violet, and it represents spirituality and enlightenment.

Then I lie there, my chakras open, and this time, I breathe in and out, breathing in a pink haze of comfort, and breathing out the black smoke of negativity.

The whole process takes about ten minutes, and I concentrate on all that's good in my life.

I've got what I've always wanted.

I'm an architect at the top firm in Denver.

It's possible I can work on the project of my dreams.

My chakras are opened, I'm relaxed, and I let myself enjoy the fact that my life is exactly where I want it.

Breathe in, breathe out, breathe in, breathe out...

The relaxing floral scent of the lavender seeps into my body, relieving the tension.

Facilitating the role of my chakras.

And I breathe, breathe, breathe...

Then I open my eyes.

Yeah.

I'm telling myself a bunch of lies. None of this is working.

When I have fewer things weighing on my mind, this exercise helps a little. It gives me something to focus on for a few minutes, offers an escape.

But once I've traveled through the rainbow of chakras, my problems are right there waiting for me, excited to start feasting on my anxiety again.

I'm sure this kind of exercise works for someone like Ashley. Colors mean more to her than they do to me. To me, they're just colors. And I have never bought into the idea that certain colors correlate to certain parts of the body and certain parts of the mind and blah blah blah. It all makes about as much sense as my cousin Ava's Tarot cards and all the heady spiritual stuff she believes in.

Me? I'm just Diana.

I'm an architect. Architecture is all about mathematics and physics. Sure, there's a creative aspect to it—one which I enjoy immensely.

But if you don't get the math and physics right, that beautiful building you designed will fall.

There's nothing spiritual about math and physics.

I stay in the tub for a few moments longer because the warmth and aroma are relaxing.

Then I step out of the water, dry myself in a fluffy white towel, moisturize my face for the night, and get into the lounging pants and tank top that I wear as pajamas.

I lied to Dragon. I don't sleep in lace nighties. I put that on yesterday morning because...

Because I wanted him to notice me. I wanted to entice him.

Admitting that consciously to myself is kind of freeing.

Now it's time to eat something.

I finished my shake, so I head to the kitchen and make myself a plate of fruit—some pineapple chunks, watermelon chunks, and a Granny Smith apple. I think about my sister, Brianna. Granny Smith is her favorite type of apple—we grow them in our orchards.

I like them too. The tartness of the apple and the sweetness of the pineapple and watermelon create a refreshing balance— my favorite combination for fruit salad.

I grab my phone to see if anyone has texted me. No one has. Not that I expect Dragon to text me. Why should I care where he is?

I set my phone down when it rings.

It's Brianna.

"Bree?"

"Hey, Dee."

"Why are you calling? Aren't you supposed to be enjoying

your honeymoon?"

She giggles. "Come on. We have to come up for air once in a while."

I can't help smiling into the phone. I'm glad my little sister found her forever. Sometimes I wonder if that's even in the cards for me.

"I just wanted to find out," she continues, "how things are going with Dragon."

Now there's a loaded question.

"He's out right now. I just got home from my first day at the job."

She gasps. "Oh my God, that's right! How'd it go?"

"It went well," I say.

"Did you get that assignment you wanted?"

I frown, looking down at the flawed blueprint on the counter. "I'm not sure yet."

But that's all I say. Just can't think about the rest of it right now.

"So...Dragon?" Brianna says.

"He's all moved in."

And he got arrested for soliciting, and he also got a weird phone call that has him so on edge we hired a private investigator to trace it. Oh, and he also gave me the best fuck of my life less than forty-eight hours ago.

But I don't say that.

"Good. Does he seem okay?"

I draw a deep breath in. "I don't know, Bree. I hardly know the guy. He seems fine. But you know as well as I do that he's hard to read. He's looking for some work to help make ends meet until you guys all get back from your honeymoons and the band starts working again."

"That's good. Jesse will be glad to hear that. Is he...staying off the sauce?"

"As far as I can tell. I took him to a party Saturday night, and he didn't touch anything."

She gasps. "You took him to a party?"

"Well, yeah. He didn't have anything to do, and my friend Teddy invited me over to her place because she had some friends in town. It's not like it was a huge shindig or anything."

"But there was booze and pot," Brianna says.

"Yeah, there was booze and pot. I told him ahead of time. But he said, and I agree, that he has to learn to deal with being around that kind of stuff. Especially here in Colorado."

"And he didn't succumb?"

"For God's sake, Brianna, I'm not the man's keeper. No, he didn't succumb. But if he does, that's not really my problem."

She's quiet a moment, until— "You're right. I don't mean to make it sound like it is. You're his roommate, not his babysitter. Jesse and I just worry about him."

"I know, sis. But you don't have to worry that he's living in a gutter somewhere because I've given him a place to stay for the time being."

"And you have no idea how much we appreciate that."

"I know you do. And we're fine. We stay out of each other's way."

Except for the time we fucked like bunnies, but I'm not going to divulge that information to my little sister.

"I'm glad you had a good day at work, and I'm glad Dragon's okay. Call me if anything happens."

"I absolutely will not."

"Diana..."

"You're on your honeymoon. Enjoy it. Enjoy your new

gorgeous husband."

She sighs. "He is gorgeous, isn't he?"

I can't see my sister because we're not FaceTiming, but I'm betting she has that just-fucked look on her face. It's sure coming through in her voice.

Damn.

I saw myself in the mirror after Dragon and I...

I'd never seen that look on myself before.

And I liked it. I liked it a lot.

"Everything's cool here, Bree. Go lie on the beach."

"Okay, sis. Ciao."

I put my phone down and continue to eat my fruit salad.

And then my phone rings again.

CHAPTER THIRTY-TWO

DRAGON

We had a ring toss and a cornhole board in our backyard when I was little.

My dad used to play with me, and because I was way too little to toss the ring from where he could stand, I got to stand nearly on top of the thing, so I beat him every time.

Then he picked me up, threw me in the air, and said, "That's my boy!"

I was four or five, and Mom was always stuck inside tending to Griffin.

Our grass was never green in the backyard. Colorado is notoriously dry, and if you don't water your grass, it dies. Dad always kept the front yard watered so it looked good to passersby. But in our fenced backyard? He didn't want to waste the money, so the grass always looked more like dirt.

That was okay with me. Little boys love dirt. I would run around in the backyard chasing bugs and butterflies and our old dog Cinnamon, who was my best friend.

She was a mutt. Looked a lot like a beagle. I loved that dog, and I was broken up when she died at the age of twelve, shortly before...

Fuck.

That's how I think about my childhood.

There's before.

And there's after.

"Here you go," my Uber driver says.

"Thanks."

I get out of the car and stand in front of the house where I spent the first eight years of my childhood.

Looks the same, except that whoever lives there now doesn't care about the front yard the way my father did. The grass is more brown than green.

The shrubs are the same, though much bigger now. The maple tree growing in front is huge, and the leaves have turned to gold and red.

I draw in a deep breath and walk to the front door.

I hate doorbells, so I knock.

A barking dog peeks its head through the window on the side of the door.

"Jacob, sit," a woman's voice says. Then she opens the door. She's young, around my age, maybe even a little younger. Pretty, but not beautiful. Her mousy hair is piled on top of her head in a messy bun, and she's dressed for comfort, not style. "Yes?"

I blink for a few seconds, unsure of what to say. Of course someone else lives here now. My parents wouldn't want to live in the house where their daughter was injured and then abducted. Where their family was irreparably broken. This whole trip was for nothing.

Or was it?

"Hi, I'm sorry to bother you, ma'am. But...I grew up in this house. I know it's a lot to ask, but I was wondering if I could come in and look around."

"Did you?" She looks me up and down. "My husband and

I just bought this house a couple of months ago."

"You did? From the Locke family?"

She shakes her head. "No, from the Garcia family." She sticks her hand out. "My name is Lily Reinhart."

I shake her hand. "I'm Dra...ven. Draven Sanders."

Telling her my name is Locke might not be the best thing, and most people look at you sideways when you tell them your name is Dragon.

"It's nice to meet you, Draven." She gestures inside the house. "Sure. Come in. Pardon the mess."

"Oh, no worries. I last lived here when I was nine, and I just happen to be in town."

A child screams from the kitchen.

Lily widens her eyes. "Excuse me for a minute. She's hungry."

I peek into the small kitchen. A brown-haired baby sits in a highchair, and when she sees me, I smile at her.

She smiles back.

"She's adorable," I say.

"Yes, our little angel loves people." Lily leans down and gives the child a kiss on the cheek. "She'll smile at anyone. This is Draven, sweetheart."

She bangs her fists on the tray of her highchair and smiles again.

Lily puts some Cheerios on the tray, and the baby eagerly gobbles them up.

"Go ahead and look around," Lily says. "I need to get her fed."

"Yeah, of course." I nod. "And thanks for letting me in, though I think all I really need to look at is the backyard. It was a happy place for me when I was little."

"Oh, sure. Go on out." She points to the screen door that leads to the back.

Once I got in here, I knew I couldn't look at my bedroom, where I had been when someone came through a window and hurt my baby sister. I sure as hell couldn't look at Griffin's bedroom, where I picked up a knife covered in my sister's blood. Where my parents found me and thought the worst of me.

Those assholes didn't believe me then, and they won't believe me now. Why the hell did I come here again? What if my parents still lived here? What exactly did I think I'd say to them?

"Jacob's out there," Lily continues, "but he won't hurt a fly. He'll probably bug you to death for pets."

"Not a problem. I love dogs." I force a smile. "And thank you again. I'll just let myself out of the gate when I'm finished."

As I walk out onto the concrete slab outside the sliding glass doors, I marvel at how trusting this woman is. I don't mean anyone any harm, but she has no idea who I am. I'm dressed fairly nicely in dark jeans and a button-down shirt, my long hair tied behind my back in a band, so I guess she doesn't think I look like any kind of threat.

The outside is much like I remember it, and in my mind, I see the ring toss and the cornhole set. The old shed is still there, but its metal doors are rusted.

There's a patio table on the old slab rather than the plastic lawn chairs that were there when my family lived here.

Again in my mind's eye, I can see Griffin in her bouncer, toddling along on the slab of concrete. I see her squinting her eyes and grimacing from baby brain freeze when I gave her a bite of my popsicle.

God, I loved her.

Tears well in the bottoms of my eyes, but I sniff them back.

I got over crying about Griffin long ago.

And I only cried about my parents once.

I give Jacob a pat on the head, and then I leave the backyard, making sure to latch the gate so he can't get out.

I stand in front of the house for a few moments, letting myself remember. The wreath on the front door, welcoming people. My mother always had a wreath on the door, no matter the season. A wreath of pink blossoms for springtime, another with dandelions for the summer. Wreaths of autumn leaves and harvest vegetables for fall, and then of course the traditional Christmas wreath.

After Christmas, it became a winter wreath, decorated with winter berries and white flowers. She had hearts for Valentine's Day, shamrocks for St. Patrick's Day, and then she started again with the springtime blossom wreath.

There was a time when my parents meant the world to me. A time when I could never imagine life without them, never imagine them turning on me.

Part of my therapy has always been to put myself in their shoes, try to understand what they were feeling the day they walked into Griffin's bedroom, found her cut up, and found me holding the bloody knife from our own kitchen.

Since I'm not a parent myself, I've been told I can't imagine the horror they must have felt seeing their baby sliced open.

Griffin lived, though I imagine she probably had a scar on her cheek from the deep cut.

How?

How could you turn your back on one child for another? I

remember being frantic. Screaming, crying that I hadn't done it.

That I would never hurt Griffin.

Didn't they notice the open window?

I don't know what they were thinking.

And I didn't look back.

Not until now.

This is the first time I've set my sights on this house since the day I left it when I was eight years old.

I never looked at anything else, either. My therapist has advised me to pull the police report from the night Griffin was attacked as well as the night she was abducted.

But I haven't.

I wasn't even sure my parents filed one the night she was attacked. After all, they thought I had done it.

But then my therapist told me what I hadn't allowed myself to consider. They most likely *did* file a police report. They would've had to in order to give up their parental rights.

The police department is closed now, but maybe tomorrow I'll drive back up here and pay a visit to the Thornton Police Department to see the records.

Or perhaps they're accessible online. That would certainly be easier.

But I can't think about any of that now.

I close my eyes and try to remember the good times at this house.

Like the Christmas before Griffin was born, when I got Hot Wheels that went upside down.

I had seen them on TV, and I wanted them, and they were there under the Christmas tree from Santa. I spent the entire day staring at my new toy, mystified by the physical forces that allowed the small cars to stay on their tracks, seemingly defying gravity.

And of course I revisit the warm memory of my father giving me my first drum after Griffin was born.

It wasn't all bad.

I walk up the block, looking at my neighbors' houses for the first time in many years. The Osbornes lived two doors down, and I used to play with their little boy, Ricky. He had an older brother, Malcolm, who was a teenager. He used to help my mom with odd jobs when Dad was working overtime. He loved Griffin and always sneaked candy to her, but he couldn't stand Ricky and me. Thought we were a pain in his ass, which we kind of were. He especially hated my drum. He always said he wanted to take a hatchet to it. Whatever happened to them?

An older couple lived a few doors down from the Osbornes. Mrs. Ortiz baked the best cookies. When we were out playing and got hungry, we'd run to her house, where she'd invite us in for the very best warm oatmeal cookies and a glass of milk. She often brought my mother homemade breads and cakes. Those were good days.

I walk out of our neighborhood and up toward the strip mall where Ricky and I used to ride our bikes and get sweets at the old-fashioned candy store.

That store is long gone, and in its place is a plasma donation center.

It's open, so I walk in.

"Hello," a receptionist greets me. "How can I help you?"

I look around. "Just wondering a little about this place."

The receptionist grabs a pamphlet. "Are you interested in donating?"

"I don't know."

"We pay fifty dollars per donation, if that spurs your interest." She hands me the pamphlet.

My eyebrows nearly jump off my forehead. "You *pay*?"

"We do." She smiles. "Fifty dollars for the first five donations, and forty dollars per donation after that."

"Is it like giving blood?"

"Sort of. Donating plasma is a process that involves extracting plasma from your blood and returning the remaining components back to your body."

"And you'll pay me for that?"

"Yeah. We're always looking for more people to donate. Plasma donations are crucial for medical treatments, including treating burn victims, patients with immune disorders, and those undergoing certain medical procedures."

Seems like a no-brainer for someone who needs money. "Sure. Sign me up."

"Okay." She hands me a clipboard. "Fill this out and bring it back to me."

I take a seat in one of the plastic chairs and read through the form. When I get to the section on previous drug abuse, I freeze.

So much for making an extra buck on the side.

I put the clipboard down on the chair next to me, and without saying another word to the cheery receptionist, I walk out.

CHAPTER THIRTY-THREE

DIANA

"Hello?" I say into the phone.

"Hi, Diana, it's Antonio Carbone."

"Hi, how are you?"

"I'm good. Just wanted to let you know that I offered your friend a job."

"Dragon?"

"Yeah. I mean, I need drumming instructors, and I suppose he's qualified."

I furrow my brow. "You mean you didn't ask about his background?"

"No. I figured you wouldn't have recommended him to me if he wasn't qualified."

"He's the percussionist for an up-and-coming rock band, so yeah."

"I'm sure he'll be great. Are we still on for Friday night?"

"Yeah, sure." I put my phone on speaker and open the calendar app. "Did we say seven?"

"Yeah, we did. See you then, Diana."

"Bye."

I look up when the door clicks open.

Dragon walks in, looking pale.

I stand up. "Hey, are you okay?"

He doesn't look at me. "Yeah."

I want to ask where he was, but how can I ask that? He's an adult. He can come and go as he pleases.

"How was your day?" I ask.

"Good." His voice is artificially even. "Yours?"

Something is up with him, but I decide not to pry.

"I'm exhausted, but it was good. I got a chance to look at that great project I want, but I found a problem in the plans, which is really strange since they all have so much more experience than I do."

He simply nods.

"What did you do today?"

"Got a job. Your friend Antonio called me. Offered me a job teaching percussion. Doesn't pay a lot, but it will help tide me over until the band gets back to work."

"That's great." I force a smile. "I'm happy for you."

He simply nods again.

Something's eating at him.

Of course, something's always eating at Dragon. The most emotion I've ever seen out of him was when he and I made love.

Scratch that.

There was no love involved.

At least I don't think there was.

"You look...tired," I say. "Can I get you some water or anything?"

"I can get it myself." He walks into the kitchen, grabs a glass out of the cupboard, and gets ice water from the door of the fridge.

Then he turns and looks at me. Glares at me. Only it's not a glare. It's more of a...lustful stare?

It's not unlike the way he looked at me yesterday before...

There's something else in his gaze right now. I can't place it. I'm not sure I want to place it.

"Diana..." he says on a groan.

I swallow. "Yes?"

"I got another one of those phone calls."

Not what I was expecting him to say.

"Oh?"

He nods. "Whoever it was says I need to call off your private investigator."

I drop my jaw. "How does he even know we hired her?"

Dragon shrugs. "Got me. Of course I tried calling the number again—it was a different number from the first one— and no one answered. It just rang and rang."

"Did you call Alayna?"

"No." He frowns. "I felt like it might be too late."

"I think we need to call her right now." I grab my phone from the kitchen counter.

But Dragon comes toward me, puts his hand over mine.

Tingles I'm not expecting shoot through me.

"Don't, please."

"Dragon, we have to let Alayna know. This is a new number she can look into."

"If there's any chance that..." He shakes his head vigorously. "I can't take any chances with this."

I look into his eyes. "Dragon, what is it that you're not telling me?"

He turns his back to me then, releasing my hand. His shoulders quiver a bit.

I reach toward him tentatively, place my hand on his upper arm and turn him around.

His eyes are glazed over. There are no tears, but

something's going on.

"Dragon..."

"No one knows everything," he says. "Not even my therapist. Not even Jesse."

"I'm not asking you to spill some kind of secret you're not ready to talk about. But if you want Alayna's help, you need to at least level with her."

"I have..." He rubs his forehead. "As much as I can, at least."

He looks so sad, so resigned. "Dragon... Where were you tonight?"

He swallows. "I went home."

I raise an eyebrow. "What do you mean? You obviously didn't go back to the western slope."

"My childhood home, Diana. I haven't been there since I was nine years old."

Odd. No one knows Dragon's backstory. I certainly don't. I never even thought of him as *having* a childhood home.

"Did you see your parents?"

He shakes his head. "They moved away long ago. After..." He shakes his head again. "I can't. I just can't."

Emotion swirls through me. I want to help him. Take that tormented look off his face forever.

But I don't know how.

So I do the only thing that I think might help.

I wrap my arms around him, pull his head to me, and kiss his lips.

And what I intended as a gentle kiss turns ferocious in an instant.

He devours my mouth, shoving his tongue inside, in a sweeping and passionate kiss.

But it's over as quickly as it started when he pulls away.

My lips are almost sore, and I bring my fingers to them.

"This isn't the answer," he says darkly.

"Then tell me." I grab his hand and squeeze it. "Tell me what the answer is, Dragon. I don't know how to help you."

He yanks his hand away. "I never asked for your help."

He's right. He hasn't asked for my help. But he took it when I offered him my family's investigation services.

And now he wants to call that off.

"You know what? Fuck off." I turn around and walk to my room. He doesn't want my help? Fine. I don't need to give him my help. God knows I have other things on my mind. This new job for one, and—

I gasp as my body is jerked around harshly.

Dragon grips my shoulders in the doorway of my bedroom.

And then his mouth is on mine once more.

Another raw and ferocious kiss, another kiss that makes my knees weak and my legs turn to jelly.

But this time I'm angry. I push at his shoulders until the kiss breaks.

"Thought I told you to fuck off."

"Fuck..." he growls. "I hate what you do to me, Diana. I fucking hate it."

"Yeah? I'm not a big fan of it either."

Then he smiles. And damn, that smile... Have I even seen it before?

"God, you're hot," he says.

I raise my eyebrows.

"Do you even have a clue of what I'm capable of, Diana? What I've been through in my life? The things I've seen?"

I whip my hands to my hips. "I have no idea because you

won't talk to me."

"And I'm not going to start talking now."

His mouth comes down on mine again. This time I keep my lips sewn shut, but he is aggressive, and he slides his velvety tongue between them.

As my knees weaken, so does my resolve.

I part my lips, and he dives right in.

We kiss in the doorway of my bedroom, and I wrap my arms around his neck, pulling him closer to me.

As the desire to help him burns in me, the desire *for* him burns even stronger.

We're going to end up in bed.

I can't bring myself to regret it. After a rough day at work, Dragon Locke might just be the salve I need.

CHAPTER THIRTY-FOUR

DRAGON

I know better than this. I shouldn't be doing this. Not to her. Not again.

But I can't bring myself to stop.

She is sparkling light in the sea of my darkness.

And this new fire I'm sensing in her? The kind that made her tell me to fuck off?

It makes me want her even more.

I taste every part of her mouth with my tongue, all her sweetness, and all this newfound defiance that she's showing me tonight.

She deserves so much better than me.

Better than a man who can't donate plasma because of his history.

Better than a man who would drown his sorrows in a fix right now if he could.

Better than a man whose parents gave him away years ago.

Better than a man who was told he was evil as a child and grew up to believe it.

She deserves someone worthy of her. Worthy of her kindness and compassion, of her beauty inside and out.

That's not me.

But I don't fucking care.

Right now, I need her. And I'm going to take her.

I back her into her bedroom. A bedroom I've never seen before.

I break the kiss so we don't stumble and then zero in on her solid oak headboard.

A headboard with rungs.

Fuck...

I'm not into BDSM. I've tried it, but it's not my thing at all. Still, I'd like to tie those thin and supple wrists to her headboard so she can't move. Can't touch me.

Even though I long for her touch. Desire it. Yearn for it.

I'm not worthy. I shouldn't let her touch me.

I narrow my gaze, meeting hers. "What would you do if I tied you to the bed? To those strong oak bedposts of yours?"

She gulps audibly.

"Or better yet, if I tied your ankles to the posts of your footboard? Your legs spread for my fucking pleasure? I could do anything to you, and you couldn't stop me."

She breathes in and then exhales. "What if I didn't *want* to stop you, Dragon?"

God, the sound of my name from her lips. It drips like blood oozing from her, as if she's a vampire, ready to sink her teeth into my flesh.

This can't be Diana Steel.

Not sweet, perfect Diana Steel.

Does Diana have a dark side?

"What if I told you I wanted to turn you over, spank that creamy ass of yours? Spank it until it's red as a beet, and then keep spanking it no matter how hard you cry out?"

This time she visibly shudders. "You want to do that?"

Do I?

I have no desire to hurt Diana. But I know from experience that most women enjoy a good spanking in the bedroom. The pleasure and the pain.

"Tell me"—she licks her lower lip—"*Dragon.* Describe exactly what you're going to do to me. Don't you leave out one single dirty detail."

I close my eyes, grit my teeth against the pulsing in my cock.

Does she have any idea what she's doing to me? What she's asking of me?

"I want to tie your wrists to two of those rungs on your headboard. With one of your silk scarves, Diana. A red one, I think. Maybe blue. Tie you so tightly that you can't escape me. So you're bound and laid out for my pleasure. Like a feast on a platter. Only for me. For my eyes. My ears. My lips and my tongue. My fingers..." I thrust my hips forward. "My cock."

She sucks in a breath. Her nipples are hard, and they protrude against the cotton of her tank top.

Fuck, she has perfect breasts. Big and round and pert, with just a touch of sag to make them fall against her chest.

"Or I'll blindfold you." I lick my lips. "Take away your sense of sight. All you'll be able to do is hear me and feel me. I may gag you as well so you can't speak. You can't cry out if you don't like what I'm doing."

This time she swallows and rubs her upper arms against the chill that is clearly overtaking her.

"Then, when you're at my mercy, I'll hover over you, stare at you, look at you as much as my heart desires. I'll bite on your lip, bite on those hard nipples. Smack your breasts until they're red. Smack your abdomen, your pussy. Spread your legs and look at that paradise between them. I will look and look and look until I can't take it anymore, and then I'll dive between your legs, suck hard on that clit, bite it."

She closes her eyes, her mouth slightly agape.

"I'll make you scream. Make you beg me to stop. Except you won't be able to beg because you'll be gagged. How does all that sound, Diana? Is that what you truly want?"

She nibbles on that full lower lip of hers, making my cock ache. "All of it except the gagging," she says. "I don't like the idea of being gagged. I have allergies, and sometimes I need to breathe through my mouth."

Jesus fuck.

She's enough to make a man go crazy.

Insane with desire, insane with the sheer need to dominate and overtake.

I'm not into the whole BDSM game. Truly I'm not. But I want every part of Diana. I want her under me, submitting to me.

I don't know why that's so important.

Maybe because she's so far above me in her station. I realize she doesn't see herself that way, but I can't help but see.

"What if I tell you I have to gag you or the deal is off?"

She narrows her eyes. "Then I guess the deal is off... Dragon."

Her eyes burn with fire when she says my name, and pinpricks erupt all over me. I hold back a quiver.

A smile tugs at her lips.

She knows.

She knows not only what she does to me, but she knows what my name does to me from her lips.

She knows too much.

This woman reads me. It's disconcerting. It's also

arousing.

How? How can Diana Steel—heiress, raised with a silver spoon in her mouth, never wanting for anything—read *me*? I'm a nobody. A man so broken. An addict.

I need to walk away. But not because she won't let me gag her. It would be a sin to cover those beautiful lips with anything.

But because—if we do this again, and if we do it the way I've described—I will drag her down into the seedy underbelly of my world.

Jesse would never forgive me. Diana is his family now.

Hell, I'd never forgive myself.

Diana is all that is good and sweet in this world—so much like my little sister Griffin was.

Is?

Which is why I absolutely cannot soil Diana Steel.

"Are you going to answer me?" Diana says.

"I don't think you actually asked a question. You simply stated that you won't let me gag you, and if I refuse to do everything to you without gagging you, it's off."

She pouts her lips. "Do you have a counteroffer?"

I look at her as if she has two heads. "This isn't a negotiation, Diana."

"Isn't it? Isn't everything a negotiation...*Dragon*?"

She lowers her voice when she says my name.

Fuck...

"I don't negotiate for sex," I say, "and neither should you. You should walk away."

She looks around. "Seems we're in my room. Maybe it's you who should walk away...Dragon."

My cock pulses against my jeans. I'm ready to explode from her words alone. No one has ever affected me like this—

and already I know no other woman will.

I have to get a grip.

I turn, walk toward the door, and—

She jerks me around with more strength than I knew she had. "I'm not letting you walk away from this, Dragon. You want me as much as I want you. I see it in those beautiful eyes of yours. I hear it when you tell me what you want to do to me. I'm up for it. I'm up for everything except the gagging. I gave you the reason why. If you can't deal with that, then fuck you."

"Fuck you too, Diana."

We glare at each other for a split second, and then our mouths are fused together, our lips sliding, our tongues tangling. Who kissed who? I'm not sure, and I don't care.

All that matters is that we're kissing, devouring each other.

And I don't ever want it to end.

CHAPTER THIRTY-FIVE

DIANA

His kisses are hypnotic.

I know better.

I know enough to take him at his word. He's no good for me.

But I know something else too.

I know that I want him. That I crave him. All of him, and especially his darkness.

I want him more than I've ever wanted a man.

When I was in college and grad school, I studied hard. I wanted to be the best architect ever. It was important for me to break away from my family's business, to forge my own path.

I didn't have a lot of time for sex, and I didn't have much desire for it either.

I wondered if maybe I was just cursed with a low sex drive.

How wrong I was.

I just hadn't found the man who made my pulse race, my knees weaken, my insides turn to mush.

God...

I never thought I'd find it in the man kissing me now.

The man who has become as important to me as the air I breathe, the water I drink.

This man—this beautiful broken man. I want to help him.

Fix him.

But can I fix what's broken? Should I even try? Because part of his beauty is in his brokenness.

It's part of what draws me to him.

In this kiss...

This amazing, magnificent kiss that is taking me to the stars.

My pussy is already pulsing, throbbing, and I know I'm wet. I can feel it against my inner thighs. I desperately want him to open up to me, but if he won't do that, I can at least have this part of him.

I can walk into the darkness with him, embrace it with him, and take us both to the stars as we do it.

Does he truly want to tie me to the bed? I'll let him. I'll let him blindfold me. I'll let him smack my tits, smack my ass.

I'm ready for it.

I'm ready to give him what he needs.

And when he's done? I'll take from him what I need.

Perhaps what we both need.

If possible, the kiss becomes even more raw and urgent. Until finally—

I push against his shoulders, breaking the kiss. Then I gasp in a breath of air.

"Had enough yet?" he growls.

"Not even close. Just need to take a breath."

He inhales as well, nearly gasping.

"Don't need to breathe," he says. "Only need you." His mouth comes down on me again.

Urgency, rawness, pure ferocity.

Do animals kiss? Probably not, but if they did? It would be like this. Pure primal lust.

I can't stand my clothes. They're a harness binding me.

I want them off. I want nothing between Dragon and me. If I could crawl into his flesh, I would.

I don't stop to think how ridiculous my feelings are.

They're not even feelings, really. They're base urges. Things I've never experienced.

Things I'm not ready to give up anytime soon.

It's him. His roughness, ruggedness, his raw masculine beauty. His darkness. I want to descend with him. Live with him there. Learn everything.

If I can't fix him, I'll stay there with him.

This time he breaks the kiss, rubbing his forehead, his breath coming in rapid pants.

He turns his head to each side. What is he looking for? I have no idea.

Don't fucking care.

Finally he returns his gaze to mine. "Bed."

I turn, walk toward my bed.

But in the next instant I'm swept off my feet, and he throws me onto my bed so hard that I bounce.

"I want to rip those clothes off you," he says.

"Do it," I threaten.

"I'm serious. I'll fucking rip them to shreds, Diana."

"Do it," I echo. "Rip them. I don't care, Dragon. Get them off me however you want."

He hovers over me, grabs my tank top, and pulls it in two with his bare hands, the cotton ripping in a jagged line down the middle.

He sucks in a breath when my breasts fall.

"Look how hard my nipples are for you, Dragon."

He growls.

"I'm wet. So wet. Rip these sweats off me. I'll prove it."

He grabs the waistband of my sweats, and for a moment I think he's going to rip them off me like he did my tank top, but he doesn't. He pulls them off my ass, off my legs, throwing them on the floor.

Only my drenched thong lies between me and my heart's desire.

He closes his eyes and inhales. "God, you smell good. Like roses and sex."

I instinctively spread my legs, letting the aroma of my cunt waft up to him.

He opens his eyes. "That lacy thong is not long for this world."

I smile.

This time he rips the thong right off me.

Then he spreads my legs, brings his face down toward me, inhales again, his eyes closed.

"Sweet cunt. Sweet Diana cunt."

God. I grasp two fistfuls of my comforter, arch my back.

Will he really tie me up? He can. I don't care. But right now, I just need his cock in me. I need to come.

I'm so ready to come.

"Your clothes, Dragon." I can sense he wants me to behave submissively, so I soften my voice and speak with a slight upward inflection. "Take them off. Please."

"When I'm goddamned ready."

I switch tactics. Maybe a switch back to the fiery Diana who told him to fuck off will do the trick.

"You want me to rip them off you the way you ripped mine?"

He doesn't answer, so I sit up, grab the opening of his

collar, and use all my strength to rip the shirt in two and send the buttons flying.

"Fuck," he snarls.

"I warned you."

He lets out a guttural laugh. "You're so fucking hot, Diana. Do you have any idea how much I want to sink my cock into you? Fuck you until sunrise? Touch every part of your body with every part of mine? Turn you over, spank that lily-white ass and then slide my cock between those ass cheeks?"

The thought of anal sex has never turned me on...until now.

"I don't see anybody stopping you," I say.

He burns his gaze into mine. "Be careful what you ask for, Diana. Because you just might fucking get it."

"I let you do everything you wanted last time, and I'm ready for it again. I told you my hard limit. It's being gagged. I'm up for anything else."

"Hard limit?"

Interesting. The way he talked I was assuming he knew a lot about BDSM. The only reason I know about it is because Ashley dabbled in it a little before she met Dale.

"Hard limit. In BDSM, it's something you won't do."

"I don't do BDSM, Diana."

"You told me how you want to tie me up. Spank me. Slap my breasts, my pussy."

His eyes grow dark. "I do want to do all of that. For the life of me, I don't know why. It's not something I do. For the love of God, I want you. I want every part of you. I want you under me, on top of me, next to me. I want to slap you, fuck you, kiss you. All of it. *All of it.* I want to drown in you. Lose myself in you. Do everything to you."

CHAPTER THIRTY-SIX

DRAGON

She doesn't react. Which startles me.

I just poured my heart and soul out to this woman. Told her everything I want to do to her, everything I don't understand about myself, and why I want to do it.

Is she truly fine with it?

"Diana."

"What?"

"Tell me to stop. You need to tell me to leave."

"I won't. I will not tell you to leave. If you want to leave, Dragon, you're going to have to do it on your own."

I rise. The two halves of my shirt still hang over my shoulders. I look down, and one lone button lies on her hardwood floor. I have no idea where the others are.

And that button...

It triggers a memory, and I find myself careening back through time.

"Mommy, Griffin ate a button."

"What?" My mother goes red in her pretty face.

"I tried to stop her. There was a button loose on my shirt. She pulled it off and ate it."

"Oh my goodness." My mother grabs Griffin, who's about two years old. "Griffin, are you all right?"

Griffin giggles.

"Dragon, put on your shoes. We have to take her to the emergency room."

"But she's fine."

Mommy shakes her head. "I can't take a chance. Why did you let this happen, Dragon?"

"I didn't." I start to cry. "She pulled off the button, Mommy. She put it in her mouth and swallowed before I even knew what was happening."

We rush to the emergency room anyway. Griffin giggles the whole way. She seems fine.

We get there, and my mom is so distraught that they let us right in.

The doctor comes in. "Your baby ate a button?"

"Yes, my son had a loose button on his shirt. I'm so sorry. I should have sewn it back on."

The doctor holds Griffin, looks in her mouth and nose. "Ma'am, she looks fine. Let me take a look down her throat. We could do an X-ray, but I think she'll pass it. You just need to check her stools."

Mommy's face is white. "Are you sure?"

"Ma'am, she's clearly not in any distress." The doctor smiles. "You probably didn't even need to come in."

"But she's just a baby. Only two."

"So she's still in diapers?"

"Yes."

"Then all you need to do is check her bowel movements. If the button doesn't pass in the next two days, see your pediatrician."

"I'd feel better if we did an X-ray."

"It's contraindicated, ma'am. There's no reason to put you or your daughter through that."

Mommy cocks her head. "It's just taking a picture. You're not putting her through anything."

"There's no reason to do an X-ray and expose your daughter to that kind of radiation when it's not necessary." The doctor sets Griffin down on the exam table. "I looked down her throat. The button has clearly passed down to her stomach. She would be in obvious distress otherwise."

Mommy stomps her foot on the floor. "I am her mother, and I want the X-ray."

The doctor sighs. "I can't guarantee that your insurance will cover it, ma'am, because it's contraindicated."

"I don't care. I want the X-ray." Then she looks down at me. "This is all your fault, Dragon. All your fault."

I was six.

I forgot about that until now.

My parents were loving other than that time.

My mother apologized to me later, after we got the X-rays, which showed the plastic button had descended all the way down Griffin's esophagus and was beginning its journey into her stomach.

A day later, my mother found it in her diaper.

But that was the beginning of the end.

Even though my parents continued to be loving, I see it now.

That was the beginning of it being all my fault.

CHAPTER THIRTY-SEVEN

DIANA

"Did you hear me?"

Dragon looks lost in thought. He's looking at me but not looking at me. It's like he's looking right through me and seeing something else.

"Do I have to repeat myself? If you want to leave, do it on your own. I'm not throwing you out of here."

Then his eyes go wide, and I see the fire within them.

They're laced with sadness but also with something that seems overpowering to him.

And it's overpowering to me as well.

A storm is raging inside Dragon Locke, and I've only begun to comprehend it. I should step away. I should be the one to kick him out. I may not be equipped to handle the tornado that's cycling inside him.

But my God... Something in him calls to me.

Emotion is coiled in my belly, threatening to spring forth into something I may not be ready for.

That doesn't matter. Because it's here.

It's here, and I can't tamp it down any longer.

Feelings, such strong feelings.

They have me anchored in place—unable to stop what's inevitably going to happen.

It's happened before, and already I know this time will be that much more passionate, that much more primal.

I reach toward him, brush the shirt off his broad muscled shoulders.

My gaze automatically drops to his pierced nipples, the massive dragon tattoo covering nearly his whole chest. The colors as they swirl together like fire and ice.

That's what Dragon is, after all. He's fire and he's ice.

He's capable of so much more than even he knows. He's a hard and passionate lover, yet he holds back.

My God... What if he didn't?

Will he truly tie me up the way he says he wants to? Will he spank my ass until it's red and hurting?

I want to know.

I want to see Dragon unleashed.

Dragon on fire.

Not the Dragon who holds himself in ice, who is afraid to let his true self out.

He thinks he's sin. He thinks he's evil.

But I don't believe it. I believe this man is good inside. I believe he did give that prostitute money, and for his good deed, he was punished.

"Why?" I ask softly.

Dragon blinks a few times, and the glaze in his eyes dissipates. "What do you mean? Why haven't I left?"

I shake my head. "Why did you give that young woman money? If you had just gone away, if you hadn't been moved by her pleas—which were probably lies, by the way—you could have avoided getting arrested."

He doesn't respond, not that I expected him to.

I stand up. "I want to understand, Dragon. I want to

understand you."

Dragon casts his gaze to the floor. "No, you don't."

"Who are you to tell me what I want and don't want?" I place my hand over my heart. "If I say I want to understand, then I want to understand. Not everyone lies."

He shakes his head. "I'm not saying you're lying, Diana. I think you think you want to understand. But if you could see inside my head—if you could see the darkness that's inside me—you wouldn't say that."

Christ, are we on this hobby horse again?

"Tell me one thing. That's all I ask. Why did you give her money?"

He draws in a breath, stares at me a moment, and then— "She reminded me of someone, okay? Satisfied?"

"Who did she remind you of?"

"Sorry. You told me to tell you one thing. I told you."

I can't argue with his logic. I just didn't expect his answer to lead to more questions.

What is his story? Why is he the way he is?

How does one become an addict?

There are about a zillion answers to that question. Not that I would know any. Dragon is the first addict I've known. I knew people in college who overindulged, but none of them were addicts. They'd go back to class on Monday and continue getting straight As, only to party hard again the following weekend.

That's not addiction. That's letting loose.

Addiction is another thing altogether. Since I hardly drink and I never took drugs—at least not knowingly—it's not something I understand. But I want to understand. Because I want to understand Dragon.

But if he won't tell me who the hooker reminded him of, he's certainly not going to indulge me if I pepper him with questions about addiction.

Dragon is a very private person, and it probably irks him that I even know he's an addict.

"Fine," I say. "I won't ask any more questions. At least not tonight. But as I said, I'm not kicking you out of here. If you want to leave, leave on your own."

"I don't want to leave," he says. His voice is low, almost menacing.

I can't help a slight smile. That's the first time he's said anything like that. That he actually wants to be with me.

"Then don't."

"Show me your silk scarves," he says darkly.

The two halves of my tank top are still hanging around my arms, my breasts totally exposed. I walk to my dresser, open the top drawer where I keep my scarves and other accessories. I choose a dark-blue one. Not because of the darkness in Dragon, but because it's on top.

I hand it to him.

He gazes at it, moves it in his hands, fingering the fabric. "You have another?"

"I do." I grab the next scarf, which is light pink.

Darkness and light.

Dusk and dawn.

I hand it to him.

He takes it, gazes at it for another minute, fingering the fabric once more.

"Lie down on the bed, Diana. Lie down and grab two rungs on your headboard."

His voice is low and dark, and for a moment, I feel like

it's the dragon on his chest talking to me. As if that's the true person he is on the inside. A fire-breathing dragon.

But he's not.

He's simply a man. A troubled man. A man for whom I'm rapidly developing feelings I shouldn't have.

It's more than just his dark good looks. Hell, I come from a family of men with dark good looks. It's more than just his gorgeous hazel eyes. Even though they're so unique, like a cascade of water falling over soft moss.

It's the beast within him. The storm-tossed animal trying to get out.

And it's focused solely on me.

It tells me to obey him. To obey him without further questions.

So I do exactly that.

I lie down on my bed, and I grab two of the oak rungs.

He ties my wrists to the rungs tightly. He doesn't ask if it's too tight. He simply does it.

I don't complain.

He'll untie me if I ask him to. He hasn't said this, but I already know he will. Because despite what he thinks of himself, he's not evil. Evil men don't give prostitutes money to keep them out of trouble with their pimps.

Evil men don't worry so much about relapsing into the darkness of addiction.

He may not be a nice man, but he's far from evil.

I can tell he's done this before, because the knots he ties show skill. I'm not actually attached to the headboard. He tied the scarf around my wrist, securing it, and then secured the rest of the scarf to the rung.

I wasn't expecting that. I figured he'd simply tie my wrists straight to the rung.

"Grasp the silk," he says.

With my fists, I'm able to grasp the length of silk between my wrists and what's tied to the headboard.

"Stay like that," he commands. "Don't move your hands."

"Are you going to blindfold me?" I ask.

"Not this time. I want you to watch everything I do to you, Diana. Watch it. See what I'm truly like."

I suck in a breath at his words. My heart's beating fast like a hummingbird's, and the pulsing between my legs has become nearly unbearable.

My pussy is soaking wet, and I desperately need him. I need his big cock inside me. But I'll be patient. I'll see what he has in mind. And I'll watch every second of it.

"I'll watch you," I tell him. "I'll watch everything you do to me. And you know what, Dragon? I'm still not going to think you're horrible."

"You may rethink that." His hand comes down on the top of my breast with a loud slap.

I gasp, my eyes wide.

"I'm not who you think I am, Diana."

"You think that scares me? You already told me what you were going to do. You haven't scared me away, Dragon. You haven't scared me away, and you're not going to."

"Don't bet on it."

He's still wearing his jeans, and the bulge in his crotch is unmistakable. Whatever he's about to do to me, it's got him turned on as all hell.

He slaps my other breast, and then he takes both nipples between his fingers and pinches me. Hard.

God, it hurts, but it's a good hurt. It makes my nerves

tingle all the way down into my pussy, culminating in my clit.

"That hurt?" he asks.

"What do you want me to tell you? That it hurts? Yeah, it hurts." I allow a grin to crack through my face. "And you know what? I fucking like it, Dragon. I like what you do to me. I like that you make me say 'fuck' more than I've ever said it in my life. I like that you're not like every other lover I've ever had. You know what? They're boring. Why do you think I'm still single?"

His eyes widen at that one.

Uh-oh. Shouldn't mention that. Does he think I'm looking for a husband? Because Dragon Locke may be a lot of things—and I may be feeling things I shouldn't be feeling—but he's definitely not husband material.

He chuckles. "So I'm not boring."

"Not even slightly. You're not boring, Dragon. You fucked me hard and you fucked me good. And you don't have to smack me around to not be boring."

"You think that's who I am? You think I like to smack women around?"

"No, I don't think that. A man who likes to smack women around doesn't give money to a prostitute to keep her from being smacked around by her pimp."

He says nothing then.

"You can try to drive me away. You may even succeed. But you haven't yet, Dragon. Smack me all you want to. Turn my whole body red. Draw blood, even. I can't stop you. I'm tied to the bed."

He sears his gaze into my body. "Be careful what you wish for, little cowgirl."

I can't help a smile at that one. "You're right. I grew up on a fucking ranch, Dragon. You think I'm afraid of a little blood? I've been tossed around by bucking broncos and angry bulls. I learned to ride a horse nearly before I could walk. I've been falling out of apple and peach trees since I was a little kid. So do your worst, Dragon. Do your worst to me."

He softens slightly.

Just as I suspected. He doesn't have any desire to hurt me. His only desire is to fuck me, to lose himself in my body. And my body is more than willing.

But then...

He pinches my nipples hard once more, and his mouth descends on mine.

CHAPTER THIRTY-EIGHT

DRAGON

My heart is throbbing like a stampede of wildebeests, and my cock is throbbing in time with their hooves. I can't believe she's lying here. I can't believe she let me tie her wrists to the bed.

It's not the first time I've done it, and it may not be the last.

But I never expected to do it to Diana Steel.

My palm still stings from slapping her breast. Her beautiful plump breast.

And as she looks at me with fire in those dark eyes, all I want to do is fuck her. Hard and fast and thorough.

Sometimes I know why I was named Dragon.

Because I become the dragon within me.

I've worked hard to tame him over the years. It's the dragon who succumbs to drugs and alcohol.

But also inside me is that scared little boy who was torn away from his home when he was only eight years old. That scared little boy whose parents abandoned him. That scared little boy who—

I break the kiss.

Diana's eyes pop open. "Something wrong?"

"No." I stand up, kick off my shoes, and remove my jeans and underwear, freeing my aching cock.

I turn back to her, and her eyes widen. She's seen me

before, but I always get that reaction from women. I know I'm large. I know I burn into a woman's pussy.

Right now, I've got Diana spread-eagled on her bed.

And a moment later, my cock is inside her.

"God yes," she grits out, pulling on her bindings. But then her eyes open wide. "Dragon, no!"

I pull out of her quickly. "What?"

"Condom."

"Fuck." I grab my jeans from the floor and pull out a condom. I hate the damn things, but she's right. Though I doubt I have anything to fear from her.

"I'm clean," I say. "They test for STDs monthly at the rehab, and you're the first person I've been with since then."

Did I just tell her that? But it's true. She's the first woman I've fucked sober. *Damn.*

"I wasn't worried about that," she says. "It's just... I'm not on the pill, Dragon. It doesn't work for me. It makes my blood pressure go sky high."

"What do you use, then?"

She shrugs. "I don't have a lot of sex. That's my birth control. I used to have an IUD, and I have an appointment next week to get another one inserted. But for now...I'm afraid it's condoms."

I slide the rubber on. And then I plunge back into her pussy.

I fuck her and I fuck her.

The sweetest and tightest pussy I've ever fucked.

How does this woman not have a lot of sex?

She's fucking paradise.

I fuck her and fuck her and fuck her until my release takes hold, and I spill, letting myself, if only for a moment, think that

I deserve to be here in bed with this beautiful woman. Inside her amazing cunt.

And though I want to look into those gorgeous eyes— something I didn't do the first time—I resist.

I resist because I don't want this to be the last time I bed her.

When my orgasm dies down, I roll off her and dispose of the condom quickly.

Then I untie her wrists.

She rubs them absently.

And though I don't ask her if she's okay, part of me worries that she's not. I doubt Diana Steel has ever been tied to a bed before.

"Turn over," I say. "Turn over and give me that gorgeous ass in the air."

I lie under her, positioning my head right below her pussy.

"Sit on my face."

She slides over my lips and chin, her pussy juices delicious and welcoming.

I lick her, eat her, grind my face into her.

Minute upon minute, I devour her, eat her pussy. Slide my tongue over her.

A moment later, I move, slide her onto her back, and spread her legs.

Then I push her thighs forward, and I slide my tongue over her puckered little asshole.

Man, what I wouldn't give to shove my cock into this tightness. Already I'm hard again just thinking about it.

But I hold myself in check, eating her, nibbling on her clit.

She moans, groans, fists the comforter, until I shove two fingers inside her.

One nip to her clit and she's soaring.

"Dragon! My God!"

I continue sliding my tongue over her, probing inside her, as her walls contract around my hand.

So sexy, so hot, so much I'm not worthy of.

But I'm in it now.

I'm in it up to my eyeballs, and though I should regret it, I absolutely don't.

She screams through her orgasm, and I continue sliding my tongue over her clit, nipping it lightly, letting the waves wash over her. When I feel her coming down, I slide back to her clit, and she erupts again.

My God, this woman...

My God...

After two more orgasms, I finally let her go. Let her slide onto her bed, become one with her sheets. And her eyes close.

This is what she needed after a hard day at work, her first day on the job.

She needed to relax. Release.

And helping her was no hardship on my part.

But I'd be a fool to think this can be anything but what it is. I'd be an idiot to think she would ever have true feelings for someone like me.

I lie next to her for a few minutes until she lets out a soft snore.

Then I grab one of the extra blankets from the foot of her bed and cover her. I grab my shirt and the rest of my clothes and walk quietly to my own room.

I look at my phone. No more phone calls from mysterious numbers. But there is one thing I know I have to do. And I will need Diana's PI to do it.

I need to locate my parents.
It's time to confront them.
Whether they want to see me or not.

CHAPTER THIRTY-NINE

DIANA

My alarm rings at five thirty a.m., and for a moment I don't know where I am.

I'm not under my covers, and I'm naked except for the tatters of my tank top still around my shoulders.

I can't think about any of that now or what it may mean.

I have to get ready for work.

Figure out how to talk to Rod about the issue with the mountaintop resort plans.

I walk into the bathroom and notice the redness on the tops of my breasts from where Dragon slapped me last night.

It was a strange sensation. Painful, yes. But also...

It was like I felt I was giving him something. Something he needed, and something I needed as well, though I didn't realize that.

I don't know what it all means, but I think we both took what we needed last night.

I would've liked for it to have lasted longer, but those three orgasms that sent me into a slumber like no other were certainly wonderful.

Ugh. All this time I was so looking forward to this job, so hoping I'd be assigned to this project.

Yesterday, all my dreams seemed to be coming true.

But today...

What am I going to do?

I could ask one of the other architects on the project rather than go straight to the boss.

Yeah, that's what I'll do.

I dress quickly today, choosing a black pencil skirt and my black, mid-heel patent-leather pumps.

A crisp white blouse completes the picture. I'm not as comfortable as I was yesterday, but I look a little more professional, and I need to be taken seriously today.

When I walk out my bedroom door and head to the kitchen, I can't help but notice that Dragon's door is closed. He's probably still sleeping. Not that it matters to me. Not that it should, anyway.

I boil some water in the microwave for my French press. Then I add spoonful after spoonful of my special Jamaican Blue Mountain blend. If there was one thing my mother taught all of us, it was to enjoy a cup of strong black coffee.

She's a coffee snob, and she turned me into one as well.

I pour the boiling water into the pot and let it sit for a moment before slowly pressing the grounds all the way to the bottom.

Then I pour myself a steaming cup.

I take some fruit out of the refrigerator and eat it with my cup of coffee. Then I grab my jacket—black leather blazer—and quietly leave the penthouse to walk to work.

I own a car, and it's in the garage in the basement of the building, but living and working downtown, I rarely need to use it. I enjoy the walk to work, even in my heels, because it's not that far. Not as comfortable as the cowboy boots I was raised in, but when I left the ranch behind, I learned to adapt.

When I get to my office, I slide my brand-new ID into the reader in the elevator and go to the top floor.

"Good morning, Ms. Steel," the receptionist greets me.

"Please, call me Diana."

"All right. Diana." She smiles. "How was your first day yesterday? I didn't see you leave."

"No, I stayed late. It was good. Thank you for asking."

She smiles and goes back to work.

I head to my workstation.

I'm trying to decide which of the architects on the project I should approach when one of them walks through my doorway.

"Hey, Diana," Marcus Luttrell says. "Just so you know, a client sent over a huge spread of bagels and pastries. It's in the small conference room if you want some."

"Oh, sounds amazing, but I already ate this morning."

He laughs, swallowing a bite of bagel. "Hell, so did I. But I never turn down free food."

I laugh lightly.

Marcus is about to leave, but I stand up. "Marcus, can I ask you something?"

He walks in my office and sits down across my desk. "Shoot."

I take a seat. "Tell me if I'm being too picky, but I was looking through all the paperwork on the mountaintop project yesterday, and I found something that bothered me."

He cocks his head. "What's that?"

"One of the pipelines." I pull out the blueprint and trace my finger along the proposed pipeline. "Maybe I'm reading the design wrong, but it seems to be a little too close to one of the—"

He gestures me to stop talking as he swallows another bite of bagel. "I know what you're talking about. Ledbetter and I have had words about it. Then I was told to shut up."

I frown. "So you agree with me. It could be a problem."

"I did some research on it." He looks over his shoulder and lowers his voice. "Yeah, it could be a problem. But it probably won't be."

I gesture to the pencil tracing I made yesterday. "But with some minor adjustments we could eliminate the possibility altogether."

He holds up a hand. "I know. But those adjustments will increase the budget by about two million dollars, Diana. And that's the problem."

"I don't think the firm is hurting for money," I say.

He presses his lips together. "No, but the more money the firm has, the better our bonuses are at the end of the year."

"Marcus, this is a huge project. People will be paying top dollar to go to this mountaintop resort for the time of their lives. They deserve to be safe and comfortable."

"And they most likely will be."

I shake my head. "This firm has to have tens of millions of dollars in reserves. I don't understand why this is such a big issue."

He rolls his eyes at me, and already I know what's coming.

I was raised with money. A fucking ranch heiress. Of course I don't think it should be an issue.

So I'm surprised when he says, "If it makes you feel better, Diana, I agree with you. But I also need my job. The firm is well protected with liability insurance."

"Any liability would be a PR nightmare."

He doesn't reply.

I sigh. "Besides, don't we have a fiduciary obligation to design the best structure possible for our client?"

"Depending on how much they pay us, yes."

"Oh, come on. You can't tell me they're not paying top dollar for this."

"No, I can't tell you that. Because we associate architects don't get to look at the books. I don't know how much we're being paid for this project. All I know is that Reynolds won't put in the extra money to tighten it up. That's what Ledbetter told me."

I shake my head. "I don't like this at all."

"None of us do, Diana, but it is what it is." He shrugs. "This is business. Corners get cut. Money is everything."

"Money should never be everything."

He narrows his eyes. "Maybe not to someone who has an unlimited amount of it."

There we go. I should've known. I open my mouth to respond, but he holds up his hand again.

"I apologize. That was out of line."

I cross my arms. "You may think I'm some spoiled little brat, and I suppose part of that is true to the extent that I've never had to worry about money. But I don't take it for granted."

He grins. "Maybe if you offer Reynolds a couple million out of your trust fund, he'll make the adjustments."

I cock my head a moment.

"Diana...I was kidding."

"I know that," I say, flustered.

I actually didn't know that, and for a split second I was considering it. I can have two million wired into the firm's account within five minutes.

But that's not really the best way to start this project.

"If you're worried about liability—"

"No. I'll be the least liable of anyone. I'm the newbie here. But this was my dream project. I didn't expect to find any issues with it."

He frowns. "There are issues with every project, Diana. We have to weigh the pros and cons, and one of the biggest pros—usually *the* biggest—is how much money we're going to get out of it. One of the biggest cons is how much money we'll lose."

I sigh. "Fine, I'll keep quiet for now. But this is eating at me, Marcus."

"Yeah, it's eating at me too. It's not the first time I've seen Reynolds cut corners, but this is the biggest project I've seen him do it on. I was taken aback when I realized it."

"Does anyone else know?"

"All of us on the project. Even Lopez. But we're all keeping our lips sealed."

"I guess you're suggesting I do the same."

He takes a long breath in before continuing. "Far be it from me to suggest anything to you. I hardly know you, Diana. Whether you carry the Steel name or not, I do know that this firm wouldn't have hired you if you didn't know your stuff. They hire only the best here, which means you're one of the best."

I sigh. "Part of being one of the best is building the best structure possible."

"You'll get no argument from me. In fact, I considered leaving over this. But they pay me a shit ton of money here, and my wife is pregnant with twins. So there you go."

I nod. I could easily quit. I don't need this job. But I *want* this job. I want to work on this dream project.

"Don't be a fool," he says, standing. "Chances are nothing will ever happen, and none of it will matter."

"Yeah."

"Besides," he continues, looking over his shoulder before he walks out the door, "you can follow every rule in the book, dot every I and cross every T, and a building could still have issues." He walks away.

I close my eyes and take a deep breath, rubbing the sides of my forehead. Marcus isn't wrong. In school, I studied myriad projects that went wrong for no foreseeable reason.

But this is foreseeable.

And everyone knows it.

I sigh and pull up my calendar for the day.

Great. At ten o'clock I have a meeting with Rod. Don't recall seeing it yesterday. He must've just put it on my calendar.

I may need a doughnut for this. I get up and head to the small conference room where the spread is set out. A great big glazed doughnut with pink sugar icing.

Perfect.

CHAPTER FORTY

DRAGON

I wake up, still smelling Diana's pussy on my face.

I take a few moments to inhale, appreciate it, infuse it into my body.

Because this day is going to be difficult.

First thing I need to do, before I go to the music store and get my schedule for percussion lessons, is call Alayna the PI and tell her I need her to back off on the investigation into Griffin.

But I have something else for her. Something the Steels may not pay for.

I need her to find my parents.

But before I ask her to do that, I grab my phone and pull up all my social media accounts.

I have dummy accounts on each one. I never post, and no one knows it's me. But it gives me the ability to search the sites.

Felix and Stefania Locke.

I can't find them anywhere.

On Facebook, Instagram, even LinkedIn. My father was a plumber. He'd be about fifty-five years old now, still of working age. Surely he should have a LinkedIn.

But nothing.

My mother Stefania—he called her Stevie—was a

homemaker. She stayed home with Griffin and me.

She sold some kind of cosmetics on the side. Mary Kay or Avon or something like that. I can't remember which.

If I could remember the name of the company she worked for, I could search for her that way, but when I put in Stefania Locke with the names I remember, I get nothing.

This was a million years ago anyway. My mother was young and beautiful, so she sold cosmetics easily. Women thought they could look like her, so they bought it in droves.

But I have no idea what she looks like now. After locking up one child and then losing another, she can't possibly still be beautiful. Inner turmoil tends to surface after a while.

I can't help but wonder... Do they ever think about me?

Do they ever regret their decision?

Once Griffin disappeared for real, why didn't they come for me? At that point, they should've known I wasn't guilty of what they thought I'd done.

After a quick shower, I throw on some jeans and a black Dragonlock T-shirt. God, I miss the band. When they got back from the European tour last spring, we didn't have any gigs for a while because Jesse and Rory were so busy with wedding plans.

I rejoined the band after leaving rehab, and we practiced sometimes, played a few local concerts, but nothing huge that paid a lot. Most of what I made went to pay off bills I had accumulated during rehab. Then we played at the big quadruple wedding at the Steel Ranch in Snow Creek.

Jesse and Rory took off on their honeymoons, and I haven't touched my drums since.

I walk to the kitchen to grab a cup of coffee. The pot is empty, and a stainless-steel thing sits in the sink.

A French press. I've never used one before, so I start a pot of coffee in the regular drip pot.

Then I look in the refrigerator. I grab a couple of slices of bread and shove them in the toaster.

I'm not very hungry anyway.

Once my toast is ready, I butter it and snarf it down with some coffee. Then I grab my phone, sit down at the small table, and call Alayna.

"Talk to me," she says into the phone.

"Alayna, it's Dragon Locke."

"Hey, Dragon, you were on my list to call today."

"Oh?"

"Yeah, just to give you an update. I haven't got a lock on that first phone number, and—"

"There's a problem," I say. "I got another call last night from a different number. They told me I need to call you off or they couldn't guarantee my sister's safety."

She doesn't speak for a moment, until—

"All right. Send me that number. But I should ask what you want to do."

"I'm torn," I say. "On the one hand, this could all be a big ruse. Someone's fucking with me. But on the other hand..."

"Your sister could actually be alive."

"Yeah."

She pauses. "I can be discreet."

"You weren't discreet enough because they figured out someone's looking."

"They couldn't know. I use the top technology in the business. No one can trace what I've been doing. Frankly, Dragon, I think they're trying to con you."

"They said to call her off. They know you're a woman."

"Are you saying it's less likely that a woman would be doing this work?"

I rub my forehead. "Of course not. But if I were some derelict..."

"Dragon, it's all right. I understand where you're coming from. There are typically more men in my line of work. If this guy was making this up and going with the odds, he'd probably have referred to me with male pronouns. I still am not sure that's enough to warrant throwing this investigation. He could still be trying to mess with you. But I'll leave the decision to you. Do you want to keep investigating?"

"Do you think we should?"

"That's all up to you," she says. "But if it were me? I'd keep on it."

"All right," I say. "Keep on it, then. I'll send you the information as I get it. But there's one other thing."

"Yeah?"

"I need you to find my parents. Felix and Stefania Locke." I give her the address of the house in Thornton as well. "That's the last known address, but they haven't lived there probably for decades."

I hear her typing on the other end. "This shouldn't be too difficult."

"I didn't find them on any social media."

"Older folks aren't always on social media, but I'll check it all out." She pauses. "This shouldn't be hard at all. I should have something for you by the end of the day."

I shove my phone in my pocket and rise, ready to leave and go to the music store when the intercom buzzes.

I push the button. "Yeah?"

"Dragon Locke?" a voice says.

"Yeah, that's me."

"There's a package out here for you."

"Okay, you can go ahead and bring it up."

No reply.

Then I wait.

Open the door, watch the elevator.

After five minutes, it's clear no one's coming up. Whoever it was must've just left the package downstairs.

I take the elevator down, head through the lobby, and say hi to the security guard.

"Where's my package?" I ask.

He raises an eyebrow. "What package?"

"Someone called on the intercom, said you guys had a package for me. I buzzed them up, but no one came."

The security guard looks toward the door of the building. The intercom is on a brick wall next to the door.

"I didn't see anyone."

"Were you watching the intercom?"

He frowns. "I don't really concern myself with people who call on the intercom. I concern myself with people who come into the building."

"I'll take that as a no."

I walk outside anyway, look around for a package.

Maybe it was just a prank. Some teens nearby who thought it would be funny to ring the penthouse, make the person living up there come all the way down to—

My foot hits something small. I look down.

And I gasp.

ACKOWLEDGMENTS

Welcome to the Sin and Salvation duet! I told you we'd see more of the Steels. These new books will be standalone duets. If you're new to the Steel universe, you can start here, or you can start with *Craving,* the first book in the Steel Brothers Saga.

I hope you all love Dragon and Diana as much as I do! They are different as night and day, but boy do they sizzle.

Thank you to the team at Waterhouse Press for keeping this world alive. Special thanks to my editor extraordinaire, Scott Saunders, and also to the rest of the team, Jon, Jesse, Haley, Amber, Michele, and Chrissie. I appreciate all of you!

Thank you to my husband, Dean (aka Mr. Hardt), my sons, Eric and Grant, and my brand-new daughter-in-law, Cally, for your endless support. Special thanks to Eric for helping me get this manuscript in top shape before it went to Waterhouse.

To my wonderful street team, Hardt & Soul, thank you for being my cheering squad. I love you all!

And of course, to all my readers—I couldn't do any of this without each and every one of you.

I Am Salvation will be here soon!

#1 *NEW YORK TIMES* BESTSELLING AUTHOR

HELEN HARDT

I AM
SALVATION

A STEEL LEGENDS NOVEL

ALSO BY HELEN HARDT

The Steel Brothers Saga:
Craving
Obsession
Possession
Melt
Burn
Surrender
Shattered
Twisted
Unraveled
Breathless
Ravenous
Insatiable
Fate
Legacy
Descent
Awakened
Cherished
Freed
Spark
Flame
Blaze
Smolder
Flare
Scorch
Chance
Fortune
Destiny
Melody
Harmony
Encore

Blood Bond Saga:
Unchained
Unhinged
Undaunted
Unmasked
Undefeated

Misadventures Series:
Misadventures with a Rock Star
Misadventures of a Good Wife (with Meredith Wild)

The Temptation Saga:
Tempting Dusty
Teasing Annie
Taking Catie
Taming Angelina
Treasuring Amber
Trusting Sydney
Tantalizing Maria

The Sex and the Season Series:
Lily and the Duke
Rose in Bloom
Lady Alexandra's Lover
Sophie's Voice

Daughters of the Prairie:
The Outlaw's Angel
Lessons of the Heart
Song of the Raven

Cougar Chronicles:
The Cowboy and the Cougar
Calendar Boy

Anthologies Collection:
Destination Desire
Her Two Lovers